Cradle of the Gods

Cradle of the Gods

Book One of the Soulstone Prophecy

Thomas Quinn Miller

To my loving wife and children.
Because of all of you, I'm a better person.

Contents

1	Life's Little Lessons	1
2	Welcomed Guests	7
3	An Evening Feast	13
4	Between Friends	22
5	Unwelcome Guest	26
6	The Culler	30
7	Elder Concerns	35
8	Returning Home	38
9	The Cost of Discordance	43
10	Redwood Village	49
11	The Three Arrows	58

12	Between a Rock and a Dark Place	64
13	The Ruins	69
14	The Dreaming	75
15	Awakened	79
16	Across the Mountains	86
17	There is More	93
18	A Heavy Burden	99
19	Journey to Lakeside	106
20	On the Horn	112
21	In Everyone's Best Interest	116
22	The Festival	121
23	The Welcome	129
24	The Manhood Tests	132
25	Discoveries	138
26	Unlikely Allies	148
27	Everything Changes	153
28	Rite of Attrition	160

29	Sacred Duty	164
30	The Rescue	169
31	His Word is Law	171
32	Sacrifice	178
33	Decisions	193
34	Best Laid Plans	199
35	On the Edge	202
36	The Cave	210
37	Inner Strength	219
38	Meeting of the Minds	226
39	Uninvited Guests	232
40	Those We Love	241
41	It is Written	247
42	To be Chosen	252
43	Goodbyes	260

Acknowledgements

A story starts out as one person's idea and grows as it is shared with others along the way. Like so many other fantasy novels, this one began on a table surrounded by friends and strewn with dice, paper and more than a few assorted soda stains. Those times were some of the best.

A big thank you to my close friend, Clane for being there from the very beginning. Your encouragement and support kept me going. You're one of the good ones, buddy. Thank you to all my other beta readers, I am grateful for the time all of you spent reading and rereading these chapters. You found the mistakes that hid right in front of these tired eyes.

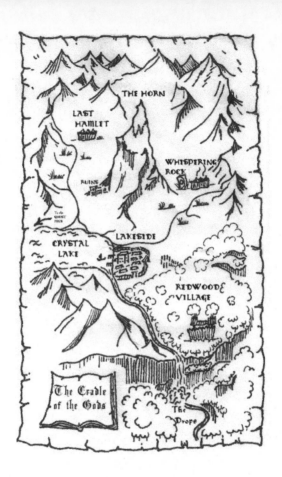

1

Life's Little Lessons

 HIS *time I'm going to die.*

Teeth flashed before his eyes. Fur covered muscle pinned him down. He shielded his face and rolled over trying to protect himself. He could feel hot breath. A scream passed his lips. This only seemed to drive the beasts on. He felt the seams in his tunic give, the last strips of dried meat falling as the seams of his pocket tore. He lay there, forgotten. The two hounds fell on their newly-freed prizes.

"If you were a wolf that would have been a fine lesson," his father called out.

"Ast! Cuz! To me!"

Ghile kept his face hidden in the grass as the two white Valehounds trotted to his father. He hesitated a moment to gather himself. Rising, he wiped his face along a soiled sleeve, trying to remove the dirt and hopefully the tears as well.

"I'm sorry," he winced, a fresh cut on his mouth. Ast and Cuz reached his father and sat obediently to either side. Ghile glared at them.

There was so much more Ghile wanted to say. Those hounds always did their best to embarrass him. It was as if they were trying to prove he would never be as good as Adon. How he missed his older brother. He knew better than to mention Adon. The loss still hung heavy on his father. Ghile could feel the weight of it between them, especially during these lessons.

"Don't just stand there staring at them like it's their fault. Gather those scraps and try again," Ecrec said.

His father stabbed the tip of his spear into the ground, then reached down and patted the two. Even sitting, their heads rose above his waist. Valehounds were bred to be big. The people of the Cradle used them to protect their flocks and homes. The wolves of the surrounding mountains would make quick work of anything less.

"Ecrec, you taskmaster. The boy was almost devoured by your beasts. I should think such a battle would earn him a rest," Toren said, giving Ghile a sidelong wink.

His uncle was always quick to smile or find humor in something. Uncle Toren was the light to his father's shadow. Father always seemed so serious, always wore a frown behind that dark beard. Ghile

2

sometimes found it hard to believe the two were brothers. But past the different expressions was the same thin, sharp nose and high cheekbones.

Ghile was thankful that his uncle had come down from the mountains for one of his visits. Uncle Toren's presence helped draw away some of his father's wrath.

"He has to learn, little brother," Ecrec said. He crossed his arms over his thick chest, leaving little doubt as to whether Ghile would get a rest. "He has seen fourteen years and is of age. He is not a child any longer. He takes the test this season. How will he fare? He cannot even command the respect of the hounds. He needs to be ready," Ecrec said. He did not look at his brother as he spoke, but stared at Ghile.

Avoiding his father's eyes, Ghile looked past the wall where his uncle relaxed. Their flock grazed stoically on the other side of the low wall, the pink of their skin barely visible from the early spring shearing. The snow white lambs frolicked near the ewes, tails wagging.

As a sheepherder, the hounds should have been obeying his commands, not knocking him to the ground and taking their rewards by force. This was just one of the many tasks he regularly failed at. His brother had always made these lessons seem so easy.

With the ending of spring, his family would soon travel down the valley to Lakeside where he and other boys from the hamlet would take their test of manhood. All the people of the Cradle gathered in Lakeside for the festival and the test.

He had often looked forward to these trips in the past. There was food and games. He remembered as a youth watching from beside his mother as Adon took his test. Adon had returned the next morning as a man.

He might even have been chosen to become a fang, a warrior trained in wood lore and tasked to protect the valley, like Uncle Toren. That is, if Adon had not been culled by the dwarves. Ghile could still see his brother being escorted into the Bastion in Lakeside. That was the last time he ever saw his brother.

He gathered the few remaining strips of meat from the grass. He went to place them in his now-torn pocket. Ghile sighed. His mother had just repaired his tunic the day before last. She would not be happy.

Holding the strips of meat in his hands, Ghile began trudging through the field to put some distance between him and the two hounds. A cool spring wind gusted up the valley, giving him an icy push. Ghile took in the fresh air, thankful for it. When the wind was still, clouds bunched together before the mountains, dumping rain on the valley. Luckily, there were no such clouds today.

There was a clear view of the snow-tipped mountains that stabbed into the sky around Upper Vale. The tallest of them stood like a dark guardian over the rest. It even jutted into the valley as if it were too important to just surround it like the others. It was this one worn and pockmarked mountain, known as the Horn, which separated Upper and Lower Vale.

4

Ghile looked farther up the valley towards his home, seeking something other than the stark ugliness of the Horn. The browns and yellows of the thatched roofs and timber palisade of Last Hamlet looked like driftwood on a lake of green. The winds set the grass rippling, only adding to the illusion. The winds raced past him and up the valley along the rolling hills and scattered outcroppings of gray rock.

His people called their sheltered home the Cradle of the Gods. How strange a race cursed by the gods should reside in a place named for their birth.

He stopped and turned. He rose to the tips of his toes and peered down the valley past the others. On a good day, he could just make out the glowing blue waters of Crystal Lake.

He knew his father's patience would be wearing thin, but he sought anything that would delay the rest of this lesson. He spotted two figures making their way up beside a squat stone wall, a pack-laden mule in tow.

The one in front was older and slightly bent. His stark white hair obvious even from this distance. The other young, with a swaggering gait. Ghile pointed and almost leaped with excitement.

"Father! Uncle! Look! It's Sorcerer Almoriz," he shouted down to them.

Ecrec and Toren both turned and looked down the valley. Ghile waited, his eyes darting from the two approaching figures to his father. He looked to his uncle for help.

5

"Well, are you going to give the boy his leave or wait 'til he bursts?" Toren said.

"I best go tell Elana and the others. The women will have our ears if we don't give them warning." Not waiting for an answer, Toren pushed himself up off the wall and grabbed his bow.

Ecrec scratched his beard and glanced down at the hounds still at his side. "To the flock, boys. We must find some old ones. We'll be having mutton tonight."

He hadn't finished the statement before the hounds darted forward and leaped the stone wall, their shaggy white shapes cutting through the sheared flock. In winter, it would be hard for a predator to see the sheep's guardians before it was too late.

Ghile needed no further urging, already running down the field past his father and uncle. He had wanted something to delay his lessons. He couldn't have hoped for anything as exciting as a visit from the Sorcerer of Whispering Rock.

2

Welcomed Guests

"**G**REETINGS to you, young Ghile," the old sorcerer said. He smiled at Ghile's exuberance.

Wrinkles seem to cover every available surface of skin, like vines clinging to the bark of a tree.

"What, may I ask, happened to you?" the sorcerer said.

Ghile realized he was staring. Quickly bowing his head, he spread his arms and displayed open palms to the sky as he had been taught when greeting an elder.

"And to you, Master Almoriz. I was, um, training with the hounds."

Almoriz nodded and glanced back at his apprentice. "I see. A lesson to be learned here, Riff. Ecrec of Last Hamlet teaches his children well. Even when bruised and battered, he still remembers how to greet an elder. You would do well to learn from his example." With that and a nod, Almoriz leaned into his walking stick and continued his climb.

Riff adjusted his sack. "I will, Master." Waiting a few moments before following, he tugged the rope to set the grazing mule in motion. He lowered his voice and whispered, "If I ever want to learn how to woo a sheep."

Ignoring the jab, Ghile fell into step, still grinning. He glanced sidelong at Riff and marveled at the changes since he saw him last spring. Ghile envied his freedom. Riff accompanied the elderly sorcerer to the villages and hamlets throughout the Cradle. "Sheep would be a step up for you, Riff. Though you will need to wash that dirt off your chin," Ghile took a couple of steps forward and rounded on Riff, straining to squint down at his face, "Or is that hair?"

Riff was shorter than Ghile by a head, even though he was five years older. Unlike Ghile's tangled brown curls, Riff's hair was straight and long.

Riff smiled and playfully pushed him aside, "So much for respecting your elders. How goes life in exciting Upper Vale?"

Ghile's smile fell. "Same as it was and will forever be."

"You take your test this season?"

Ghile nodded. "Yes, but father has made it clear his remaining son is to be a sheepherder."

Riff took a moment to reply. Ghile knew it was the way he had said 'remaining son'. Riff and his brother Adon had been close friends. Ghile had never spoken to Riff about Adon after his culling, but ever since, they had naturally gravitated towards each other on his visits.

"Even if you're chosen to be a fang like your uncle?" Riff said.

Ghile could only smirk.

"I am sure the druids will be falling over themselves to declare you a fang. I think they will take one look at you and think a fang isn't good enough. They will declare you a shieldwarden of one of the druids."

Ghile didn't respond. The idea of him being chosen to be a fang by the druids was ridiculous enough, but only the bravest fangs were bonded to one of them and declared a shieldwarden.

The druids were the spiritual leaders of his people and along with their shieldwardens and fangs, like his Uncle Toren – their guardians. The Cradle lay too far on the borders of the dwarves' kingdom to warrant more than a small dwarven outpost and they rarely patrolled beyond the walls of Lakeside; his people needed to protect themselves. He would be lucky to survive the test, let alone be noticed by the druids.

The two followed behind Almoriz for a while in silence. Ghile didn't want to talk about the test or the druids. It was bad enough he was going to have to go through it, knowing it really made no difference to his future. He could see it laid out clearly before him; a long boring life leading to nothing but the passage of time in Upper Vale.

"I see you have added some new pouches to your belt."

Riff wore the knee length tunic favored by men of the Cradle, but unlike others, the leather belt he wore was covered in numerous pouches and bags. Ghile recalled Riff explaining those pouches held all the components a sorcerer needed to practice his craft.

Riff nodded and absently touched one of them. "I am working with metals now."

Ghile thought back to what Riff had told him on previous visits. There were few humans with the innate ability to wield magic. Almoriz and Riff were the only sorcerers Ghile had ever met. He only knew of one other in all the Cradle.

He didn't really understand everything Riff had tried to explain, but knew sorcerers were born with their abilities and you could not become one simply by being taught. The magical spark, as Riff had put it, had to be there, then be nurtured and strengthened.

A sorcerer could force his will on the environment, making it change to his desires. They could create fire that would burn for months and never blow out. They could hone and sharpen metal and even make it stronger. Ghile especially liked when Riff would entertain his little sister, Tia, by making water dance and take on the shapes of animals.

But Riff had also confided a sorcerer needed to touch a small token of whatever he affected. Riff called it the source. The part which really surprised Ghile was that the source was consumed in the casting. Regardless of whether he was able to understand, he knew that was the way of it.

So, Riff carried various 'sources' in all those pouches and bags. Apparently, now including small pieces of metal.

"Where do you get the metal?"

Metal was a rare thing among the people of the Cradle. Only their dwarven overseers knew the secret of coaxing it from the ground; a secret they guarded closely.

Ghile knew some metals were worth more than others, but did not truly understand the differences. He knew the coins the dwarfs traded in and the spear tips and knife blades his father traded for, were different types of metal. But, it would be costly indeed for a sorcerer to work his magic on metals when he would consume some in the process.

Riff smiled and raised his eyebrow with an air of superiority. "We sorcerers have our ways."

"Now you sound like one of the druids," Ghile teased, knowing how Riff felt about the druids.

Riff took the bait. "A sorcerer is nothing like a druid. We do not beg the All Mother for her favor through song and dance. A sorcerer makes the changes he wishes, not through pleading to the mother of the gods like a child wanting a biscuit."

"Riff! That is enough!" They both flinched at the sorcerer's tone. Ghile hadn't realized Almoriz had been listening. Behind them, the mule took advantage of the stop and started grazing again.

"I have warned you before about disrespecting the daughters," Almoriz said, his visage stern. "The druids deserve the respect they receive. How many times must I remind you it is through their pleading, as you put it, that the dwarfs even suffer us to exist? Have I not taught you the histories?"

Riff lowered his eyes. "Yes, Master Almoriz, you have."

"Well then, take them to heart as you do your other lessons and mind that tongue of yours." Almoriz stared at them both for a moment longer before turning and continuing up the path.

They followed in silence.

3

An Evening Feast

NCLE Toren had been right. Ghile's mother, Elana, had broken into one of her contagious smiles when she heard the news, and it quickly spread on throughout Last Hamlet.

Lower Vale and the village of Whispering Rock lay down the valley and on the other side of the Horn; a two-day journey. The sorcerer's visit not only allowed the old Tinker to use his magic to mend pots and sharpen steel like no hammer and anvil could, but also brought news from the rest of the Cradle.

The buzz of activity they walked into reminded Ghile of festival days. They passed under the stout wooden gate of Last Hamlet and the sound of the wind was replaced with excited laughter and the shouts of his kinsmen.

Ghile couldn't help but walk taller when he entered Last Hamlet. Not only was he with his uncle, a fang of Upper Vale and his father, the clan leader, but also the Sorcerer of Whispering Rock and his apprentice. He imagined himself as a hero, returning home after a great adventure.

His imaginings were shattered when his mother appeared, kissed him and ruffled his hair. She fussed over his torn tunic, then sent him on the first of the many chores he needed to do to help prepare for the welcoming feast his father would be expected to host.

Ghile's cousin Gar and his ever-present shadow, Bralf, leaned against a nearby sheepfold. Gar was one of those boys who was good at everything and knew it. Bralf, with his piggish eyes, was the type of follower those boys attracted. Ghile couldn't understand how he could be related to the likes of Gar. They watched Ghile approach, their intentions obvious.

Growing up, Adon had protected Ghile from Gar's bullying. Since Adon's culling, Gar had made up for lost time. Ghile decided to change paths and take a longer route to his father's house. In his haste to avoid the two, he tripped over his feet and stumbled. Their laughter chased after him, but luckily they didn't follow.

Uncle Toren delayed returning to his patrols around Upper Vale for another day to enjoy the celebration. He normally only stayed a couple of days. Ecrec tapped a cask as the older men gathered around it, calling for Toren's famous tale about the frost wyrm on the Horn. They had heard this tale so many times, most could tell it themselves. Many of the younger men nearby, who were butchering and preparing the coming meal, stopped their banter to better hear.

The women gathered at Ecrec's roundhouse with armfuls of the things Elana would need to prepare her home. The younger girls brushed the loose dirt off the hard packed floor, while others followed behind sowing fresh straw and giggling amongst each other about how handsome Riff was.

Woolen rugs of every color were spread around the central hearthstone, with enough room separating them to allow the women to move freely between them while serving. They brought along extra bowls and mugs, then gathered around the hearth and baking oven to cook and gossip.

As the last light of day slipped behind the wind-buffeted palisade of Last Hamlet, the men sat around the central hearth of Ecrec's roundhouse, the fire's flames casting light off the red wattle and daub walls and sloping thatch ceiling. Every rug around the hearth was taken. Young women moved among them, filling bowls and mugs, correcting those men whose stories became too outrageous. The older women and children sat along the walls, sharing stories and laughter.

Ghile and his little sister, Tia, had been sure to get a seat near the baking oven to enjoy its lingering heat. He marveled at how bright his father's home was with the torches Almoriz had freshly enchanted with everflame. How they burned so brightly, and yet wouldn't set the thatch aflame, baffled Ghile. Riff had even enchanted some this time, which only set the girls more aflutter.

Ghile shook his head at all the festival dresses his cousins wore and the dazzling displays of hastily-gathered flowers woven in their hair. Ghile wondered if Riff realized the danger he was in.

"My Sabritha is sure to catch his eye. She is of handfasting age as of this summer festival, you know," Ghile overheard his Aunt Wirt say.

"I would not want my Tera to marry a sorcerer. No telling where she would end up. Lakeside with those Dwarfs and them stone buildings of theirs. Or worse, he might take her out of the Cradle altogether. I made sure to snatch every flower she had in her hair this afternoon," Aunt Jilla added.

Ghile glanced over along the far wall at Tera. She sat there, sullen. He would be thrilled at the chance to see the world outside the Cradle.

Ghile was savoring his pottage. Normally it was mostly gravy and tubers. His father had made sure tonight's had plenty of meat. He eyed the last chunks in his bowl and then saw Tia's large expectant eyes beyond the rim.

She showed him her empty bowl. How could someone so small eat so much and stay that way? With a sigh, he handed his bowl to her and then leaned forward to better hear the adults.

"How go your studies, Riff?" Toren asked, accepting a bowl of pottage from Elana.

"They go well, Fang Toren. I'm working with metals now."

Ecrec grunted. "Good, maybe next time you visit I will barter with you to sharpen my steel and mend Elana's pots instead of your Master. He eats twice as much as anyone I know."

The others laughed. Almoriz only smiled and placed another handful into his mouth.

"Don't tease, husband," Elana scolded. "Good Master Almoriz has a healthy appetite, is all." She moved behind the sorcerer, refilling his ale.

"So tell me, Master Almoriz, what other news from the Cradle?" Ecrec asked, smiling at his wife.

Master Almoriz lifted his mug in thanks to Elana. "I have already told you of the Whispering Rock Brewsons and the casks they are preparing for this year's festival."

"News from Redwood is the same. The Fangs of Redwood speak of Vargan encroaching farther up into the mountains. Some were spotted near the lakes of the Southfalls themselves."

There were mutterings amongst the men, and the women pulled their children closer.

"I wonder if some of the Vale Fangs will be asked to travel south after the festival to help?" Toren said.

Almoriz nodded and continued. "Perhaps. They already have enough trouble to deal with in the Drops. The plainsmen raid further and further into the mountains every spring. Though I should think Mother Brambles will keep some of her druids and their shieldwardens in the Cradle after the festival, to help in the south."

"What of Lakeside?" Ecrec asked.

"Lakeside is no different than you remember it from last year's festival. I do not tarry there longer than I need to." Almoriz waved his hand before his face, as if he had caught some foul smell.

It was well known Master Almoriz had no love for their dwarven overlords, whose stronghold was centered in Lakeside, and more importantly the Sorcerer of Lakeside. Ghile heard he was more dwarf, than human. He took the coins the dwarves used in barter for his services. Other humans in Lakeside had even adopted the practice. Many thought this was too much like the dwarves, and men like the Sorcerer of Lakeside were forgetting the traditions.

Almoriz traveled among the outlying settlements using his powers to help them and only asking the freedom to come and go as he pleased, a warm place to rest, food while he stayed and enough to last him until he reached his next destination.

The sorcerer motioned his cup towards Ghile. "Will your boy be taking his manhood test this season, Ecrec? He finally looks of age."

A hush fell across the gathering. Ghile could feel his father's eyes upon him. He pretended to watch his sister, who was licking the last morsels from his bowl. Toren had brought this very subject up on his return to Last Hamlet and the shouts coming from Ecrec's house could be heard from outside the palisade.

"He will be there as is his duty. He and the rest from Last Hamlet who are of age," Ecrec said in a strained voice.

"I'm sure he will do well, he is a fine lad," Almoriz replied.

"As long as his feet stay out of his way!" Gar said.

Laughter mixed with embarrassed gasps as heads turned to see others' reactions. Gar and Bralf sat away from the wall so as not to be with the children, but still far enough from the men since they too, still had to pass their manhood tests.

Ghile saw his father's jaw tighten and then heard Bralf's guffaws silenced when Gar's mother, Aunt Jilla, hurried over and cuffed Gar upside his head.

"Mind your tongue, boy! You dishonor your Uncle Ecrec with such talk. He has shared his hearth and food."

Gar's father, Dargen, took this opportunity to drain his mug and thus avoid the entire situation.

The awkward silence was broken when Toren released a loud belch. "That meal was fine, Elana. It is times like this I wish I had not been chosen to be a fang and had snatched you or one of these other beautiful women up for myself."

Ecrec harrumphed and the others laughed when Elana bounced a chunk of bread off Toren's head.

With the tension broken, Tia climbed into her mother's lap, "Show me the water animals, Riff!"

Riff sighed, as if reluctant to appease the children. He then smiled mischievously at Tia and rose to fetch a wash bucket sitting near the hearth. The children, and a couple of the older girls, shrieked with glee. The adults dug out pipes and pouches. Then, they too settled in to watch. A show of magic was enjoyed by all ages.

Riff sat the bucket before Tia, its contents sloshing gently. He scooped a small amount of water into one hand. Stepping back, he waved his other above the first while chanting under his breath. Ghile couldn't hear what he said, but it had a rhythm to it and the words seemed more like a rumbling tone than anything discernible.

Tia leaned forward, her eyes transfixed on the top of the water. Ghile turned his attention there as well when the children began clapping and whispering with excitement. The watery shape of a small lamb rose, the water flowing across its surface. Three more soon joined it. They began moving within the confines of the bucket. Feeding on the surface and raising their heads to bleat silently.

A large wolf appeared on the surface opposite the sheep and then charged across the water. One of the children screamed. Suddenly, one of the sheep rose up to reveal itself as a Valehound, like Ast and Cuz, hidden amongst them, to attack the wolf. The children all cheered at this turn of events and then the watery figures collapsed back into the bucket.

Tia looked up at Riff with surprise. Riff shrugged and raised both of his hands to show her. They were both completely dry.

"All out of water, little one."

Tia clapped and bounced in her mother's lap, "Again! Again!"

"Your control of water is getting better, Apprentice." Almoriz drew a small stick from the fire to relight his pipe. "Your source is lasting you much longer now."

Ghile watched Riff straighten a little under the praise. "Thank you, Master."

"Again, Again!" the children demanded.

"Alright, flowers, but then it is off to bed, I should think. It grows late," Elana said.

"I would like to have Master Almoriz and Master Riff look to a few more of my spears before they retire. I also want to know what you want for that cauldron I saw in your packs, Master Almoriz," Ecrec said.

Almoriz inclined his head to Ecrec.

Toren clapped his hands together. "And I want to hear some music. Go collect your drums and pipes, men. Ladies, prepare yourself. Once the children are tucked away, I want to dance!"

4

Between Friends

HILE lay silently staring into the darkness overhead. The young ones had been taken to one of the quieter roundhouses to sleep. The music and dancing had lasted long into the night. Little by little, yawns preceded goodbyes and the families eventually left and with them, the heat.

Ghile pulled the woolen blanket up to his neck and wriggled deeper into his straw-stuffed mat. He sniffed. He would need to re-stuff the mat in the morning.

"By Daomur's beard, this straw is itchy! I will never get to sleep," Riff whispered near him, breaking the silence.

"Neither of us will, if you keep complaining," Ghile said.

Ghile listened to Riff shifting around trying to get comfortable. He heard a low, throaty growl.

"And what is with these hounds? Get off me you smelly beasts!" Riff pushed against Ast and Cuz who seemed to have taken a liking to their newest guest. "I sleep in an inn when we travel to Lakeside. An inn!" Riff said, having given up on trying to move the enormous Valehounds.

Ghile thought back to his many trips down out of the valley to Lakeside. The thought of all those buildings huddled together made him uncomfortable. His father felt the people of Lakeside had given up too many of the old ways to adopt to the ways of the dwarves. The people of Last Hamlet always camped outside the town wall when they visited for the festivals.

"I don't even know why Master Almoriz feels the need to come all the way to the top of the Cradle. Why do you live this high up? Do you even realize how much colder it is up here?" Riff said.

Ghile smiled in spite of himself. "My father says something about the grass up here being lusher for the herds. I don't know. Our family have always lived here. Last Hamlet is our home."

"Properly named, that's for certain," Riff said.

Ghile turned his head towards the central hearth where the old sorcerer lay covered in blankets. "Get any louder and you can ask him yourself," Ghile said.

Riff sighed.

"I don't see how all your complaining is helping. Sometimes you just need to make the best with what you have." Ghile shook his head at giving advice he knew he should follow himself.

"Is that your advice, prisoner of Last Hamlet?" Riff said.

Ghile rose up on an elbow and looked over to the other side of the roundhouse where his parents slept. He listened for the deep rumbling of his father's snores before replying, "Do you think I want to be a sheepherder? I would cut off my right arm to be a sorcerer."

"Make casting hard," Riff said.

"Very funny. You do not realize how lucky you are. I have lived here all my life. At least when I was younger, I had Adon."

When Riff didn't immediately answer, Ghile lay back down.

"How long has it been?" Riff eventually said.

"How long has what been?" Ghile said.

"You know, since he was, um, culled." Riff's voice was soft, almost too soft to hear.

"Four summers ago," Ghile sighed. "Things are so different now. They still will not tell me why the dwarves culled him."

"The dwarves do what they have to, Ghile. You know the histories. Surely your parents told you the histories?" Riff said.

"Some. Father doesn't care for the dwarves or their rules," Ghile said.

He remembered some of the stories about the war between the gods. His people believed all the gods were the children of the All Mother, Allwyn, as she was known by his people. Allwyn created them and they in turn each created the different races.

"We are a cursed race, Ghile. They must cull any of our kind who show any signs of the Hungerer, for fear of the second coming," Riff said.

Haurtu, the Hungerer. The insane god who tried to eat all his siblings. A story to scare children into listening to their parents.

"I have heard it said the dwarves of Lakeside pay the cullers to take those not in their favor," Ghile said.

Riff sat up at this. "Your people should be careful; that sort of talk is dangerous."

"Who is going to hear them? We live at the top of nowhere, remember?" Ghile said, then continued, "Besides, Adon showed no such signs. What signs? Did you see any such signs? Do you even know what they are?"

Ghile heard shuffling and coughing from somewhere nearby. He didn't realize how loud the sound of their voices had risen.

They both settled back down and lay there in silence for a long time before Riff replied in a low whisper.

"No, no I don't. But, that doesn't mean the cullers don't."

5

Unwelcome Guest

AGISTER Obudar hurried through the arched hallway. He closed his eyes and exhaled, trying to regain control of his emotions. He had lived among these humans too long. Adjusting his shoulder plates over his robe, he continued up the stairs to the Bastion's roof.

The rest of his clansmen were already there.

"The culler has not yet arrived, Magister Obudar," Getchkin said, inclining his head and stepping slowly backwards as Obudar swept past.

Obudar looked to the skies, squinting out the light his bushy eyebrows didn't already block. "Do not use that word, Getchkin, son of Glern. Knight justices do not appreciate the title humans give them."

Getchkin bowed again, this time lower.

Obudar looked out over the stone battlements at the surrounding human settlement of Lakeside. Fishing boats plied Crystal Lake beyond the uniform rows of wooden longhouses. A cacophony of noise pushed up from below, the humans preparing for their summer festival.

Obudar, like most dwarves, did not understand the pleasure humans drew from their incessant celebrations. Though, if he had to make a comparison, he felt it was equivalent to the pleasure he received from a season's trade fairly concluded where all parties were content. He had to admit, their festivals were good for business.

He thought about his past two decades as magister of the human containment here in the Cradle. He was proud of his record. Under his guidance, and Daomur's justice, they had produced a steady supply of goods for the empire. Cradle wool was of the finest quality and even the humans' ales and beers were beginning to demand a price comparable to their own dwarven spirits.

He had faith in Daomur and rarely questioned the laws passed down from the Judges Council in far off Daomount. He understood the dangers they felt the humans posed and the need for the Order of Knight Justices. Yet, he still did not look forward to these annual visits.

The knight justice would arrive, endure the humans' manhood tests and celebrations and then perform the ritual of attrition on the supplicants. Hopefully none of his charges would be selected for removal. Humans were such emotional creatures and never understood the need for it, even when you explained it to them. It was bad for business.

A loud screech alerted Obudar to the knight justice's arrival. The gathered dwarves watched as a large griffon and its rider came into view. The two circled over the town, taking a wide route before gliding down onto the Bastion's flat tiled roof.

The griffon's talons clicked loudly on the smooth granite, in sharp contrast to the muffled thuds of its rear padded leonine paws. White tipped wings flexed convulsively before tucking themselves neatly against its body. Reaching down from his saddle, the knight justice patted the griffon behind the wing where her golden tinged feathers gave way to the sleek hair covering the rest of her. The muscles controlling her wings went taut beneath his riding glove, the only part of him not covered in metal.

Obudar was ever impressed by these creatures. Why Daomur bestowed these magnificent beasts upon these knight justices was beyond him. Perhaps it was in compensation for their hard role in life. He did not look on the life of hunting down the progeny of the Hungering God with any semblance of fondness.

"His word is law," the knight justice called in greeting. He disengaged the riding harness with a practiced slam of his leather covered fist. The griffon lowered her head at the action and in one swift movement the dwarf swung his leg over and slid down.

"His word is law," the other dwarves responded.

"Thank you, Safu," the knight justice said. He stroked the griffon's muscled neck. "You have brought me to my destination in safety and comfort. I thank you."

The knight justice unstrapped a large, intricately detailed hammer and pack from the griffon's riding saddle.

"Go now and hunt. Return at my call."

With that the griffon took to the sky, its muscled wings lifting it in powerful sweeps.

The armored dwarf turned to address them. "I am Knight Justice Finngyr," he said.

Obudar stepped forward before him and bowed his head. The others followed his example, but bent at the waist as was required by their lower station. Keeping his eyes on the intricate bas relief carved in the knight justice's greaves, Obudar responded.

"I am Magister Obudar and these are my clansmen and council. We welcome you, Knight Justice."

The knight justice harrumphed and walked past the bowing dwarves. "I'm sure you do. Show me to your shrine. I must give thanks for my safe arrival."

He stopped at the doorway and grimaced. "This place stinks of humans. How do you stand it?"

Obudar glanced at his clansmen and read the trepidation on their bearded faces. The knight justice, having not waited for an answer, was already disappearing down the stairway.

Obudar rose to follow, the furrows on his face deepening.

Bad for business.

6

The Culler

NTER," Finngyr said.

The stout, reinforced door creaked open and a young dwarf with a beard that barely cleared his chin stepped in and bent almost completely over. "His word is law. I am here to serve, Knight Justice."

Finngyr eyed this new arrival. He was probably one of the merchant's apprentices, an accountant, if the ink smudges on his thick fingers were any indicator. "Shut the door and help me out of my armor," Finngyr said.

The young dwarf hastened to comply.

"What is your name, citizen?" Finngyr raised his arms to allow access to the strap's buckles.

"Bjurst, Knight Justice."

"Start with the pauldron straps, Bjurst," Finngyr said. "You will also tell Magister Obudar I will not be waited on by humans."

Finngyr had wasted no time upon finding the old human servant in his quarters. Without saying a word, he'd grabbed him by the back of his servant's tunic and thrown him out into the hallway.

"Of course, Knight Justice. Um, the pauldron is?" Bjurst said, fumbling with the many buckles and straps.

"My shoulders, beardling." Finngyr went on, "That includes my meals, I doubt they could make a poison strong enough to affect me, but I am not fond of indigestion."

Bjurst's eyes widened. "None of the cradlers would poison us. They—"

"Cradlers? You mean humans, beardling, humans," Finngyr interrupted.

"Er, yes, Knight Justice." Bjurst removed the pauldrons and placed them on the display stand near the bed.

"You have lived too long on the edges of the empire, Bjurst. Never trust a human. No better than goblins. Any of them could be the instrument of the Hungerer's return." Finngyr smirked.

Bjurst, swallowing hard, removed the chest plate with some difficulty. The young dwarf carried it to the display stand near the bed, but was obviously struggling with exactly how to hang it.

Finngyr let him squirm for a moment. "Well?" Finngyr said.

"Oh, I'm sorry Knight Justice, I was having difficulty hanging your armor," he said, obviously not paying attention to what he was doing.

Finngyr scowled. "Place it on the bed. I'll hang it later. As I was saying, never trust a human. At least the humans of the Nordlah Plains present themselves as they are. Proper savages. One can at least respect their honesty." He waved his arms around him. "These humans, these cradlers, as you put it, pretend at being subservient. I don't know how I got assigned here for their culling."

Bjurst looked down and cleared his throat. "You mean the Ritual of Attrition, Knight Justice?"

"I mean what I said, beardling. Do not presume to correct me. Their culling. Call it what you will, but I do not shy away from the word or the title. I am a culler of these humans." Finngyr flexed his thick fists, each one as large as a smith's hammer and as solid. "I understand these humans here accept Daomur's law without argument?"

Bjurst nodded. "Oh, yes, Knight Justice. They know and follow the laws."

"Too bad," the culler responded, removing a vambrace. He strode over to the arched doorway leading onto the room's small balcony. Finngyr felt his jaw instinctively tighten as he stared out over the humans' sharp angled longhouses. He still did not understand why he had been assigned here. This was his first assignment anywhere but the plains. This place was so docile, only one culler was needed to

32

carry out the Lawgiver's justice. He had prayed on this, but Daomur deigned not to share his reasons.

He removed another vambrace, handing it to Bjurst. Finngyr noted it still held the sheen the initiates of his order had brought out of it back in the capital city of Daomount only a few days prior.

He recalled how the plates of his armor had reflected the light shining through the white arches. The temple's main chamber sat on the summit of the mountain city, allowing an unobstructed view of the sun as it hovered over the ocean. Sweet smelling winds, tinged with sea salt, ruffled the many banners bearing the hammer and balanced scales of their deity.

Finngyr used his peripheral vision to glance at the rows of his fellow knight justices. He could sense the presence of the hundreds he couldn't see lined up behind him. Never was he more filled with the honor of his sect than during the Blessings.

Every knight justice stood rigid and straight. Before them they held their war hammers, each a relic passed down through generations of warrior priests. Much like themselves, relics from an earlier time. Once they had numbered in the thousands. Those gathered here were all that remained. Those priests chosen by Daomur to seek out and cull those cursed by Haurtu; the Hungerer, the Fallen One.

The temple was silent, except for the creaking of leather and rustle of well-oiled chainmail. All could hear the shuffle of the high priest's robes as he ascended the marble steps of the central altar. The ancient dwarf turned and faced them. "Daomur is the truth and his word justice!"

Their reply shook the very stones. "Let our hammers deliver his truth!"

"It is time to deliver his judgment. Go forth! Find the Fallen One's chosen and destroy them else their powers grow. Haurtu must not be freed. Daomur's word is truth!" the ancient dwarf intoned.

"His word is truth," they shouted in unison.

The sound of armor clanging off the floor jarred Finngyr out of his reverie. He turned to see Bjurst hastily retrieving the piece which had slipped from the bed.

"It seems you are going to learn the art of polishing armor, beardling," Finngyr said.

7

Elder Concerns

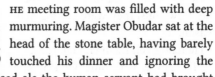HE meeting room was filled with deep murmuring. Magister Obudar sat at the head of the stone table, having barely touched his dinner and ignoring the mug of spiced ale the human servant had brought right before the room had been sealed and locked.

All the merchant clan's elders sat around the table. They now complained to one another, having tired of complaining to him. At least they all seemed to be able to agree on one thing – the most recent knight justice was going to be bad for business.

Elder Fjorn, the head accountant, was still complaining about losing Bjurst, one of his apprentices, to the knight justice as a personal servant.

"Apprentice Bjurst is my most talented pupil and his skills are sorely needed to enter the tithing. If he thinks I am going sit out there and do the job of an apprentice, he has another thing coming!"

Obudar did not remember the last time he had seen the business end of Old Fjorn's wagging finger or those wiggling eyebrows. At one point, Obudar thought they had come to life and were trying to escape off the old dwarf's face, having tired of his complaining as much as Obudar.

He would let them complain for a little longer and get it out of their systems. He considered the ale again and finally decided it couldn't hurt. Maybe it would settle his stomach. He swallowed a few deep gulps, no need to drink it too fast. A Whispering Rock brew. Good head on this one. He had to hand it to the Brewstons, they were getting better with every season.

He had given them enough time.

"The law is with him," Obudar said, causing the deep murmuring to slowly trail off like gravel coming to rest at the bottom of a gully. "We cannot interfere with the Rites."

Old Fjorn raised his finger and shook it at him yet again. "And what will the magister do when he culls half of the Cradle in his religious fervor?" The statement was greeted with many nods.

That was the meat of it. They could deal with all the other issues easily enough. The knight justice had no interest in leaving the Bastion before the Rite, so they didn't need to worry about him causing trouble in the streets. They had already instructed the Bastion's Overseer to keep the human servants away from his rooms and that food would be seen to. The real question was the Rite itself.

Obudar tugged at the edges of his beard as he considered his options.

"Why did the Guardians send a knight justice who has been assigned to the Nordlah Plains?" Elder Rawson said. "Do they want an uprising? We are not properly manned for that. All of the outlying settlements will be here and the auguries are foretelling record attendance."

"We will need the druids help," Obudar said. If they could convince the druids to help keep the peace, they might be able to avoid a disaster. The humans respected the druids and followed their teachings. He knew the druids would want to keep the peace as much as they did.

"Mother Brambles has not been seen for some time," Elder Pricedar said, adjusting his spectacles as he always did when stating the obvious.

Obudar nodded. They would need the old druid leader. Her towering cave bear alone would be enough. But, there was no telling if she would be there for the ceremony. She did not always attend.

"Have a watch set. I want the first druid to arrive brought before me," Obudar said. That would have to do if Mother Brambles herself didn't show. The Elders nodded and a number of smaller discussions on the many other matters of the day's business ensued. Obudar stared into his cup.

Would the druids help?
Would it be enough?

8

Returning Home

E *are going to cause an uprising.*
Gaidel followed closely behind her
shieldwarden. She had to return to the
Cradle as she had been told, but she
didn't believe Mother Brambles understood what
she was asking.

They made their way through a portion of the
Redwood her people simply called the Drops. Heav-
ily forested and plagued with dank ravines and tiny
rivers which snaked down from the mountains that
held the Cradle above them like a small prize. It was
the lowest part of the forest that bordered the Nordlah Plains and thus the most dangerous.

The two travelers worked their way along one of
those ravines. She paused on a patch of level ground
to catch her breath and wipe bits of mud and moss
from her thin hands. The sun didn't reach into the

deep ravines and the spring thaw still fed the icy waters that trickled through them.

Two Elks seemed to sense she was no longer behind him and stopped. The large kite shield, the mark of a shieldwarden, looked so small on his back.

"The daughter is tired," Two Elks stated more than asked.

"I am not tired," Gaidel said, trying to get her breathing under control. True, he was setting a grueling pace, but she was not going to give him the satisfaction of admitting it.

She looked around. "I was just wondering if this was the best way." It had been over two years since she left the Cradle, but she recalled being escorted down a proper trail. She was only ten and four years when she was selected to become a sister of the order, but she didn't remember having to climb down sodden ravines. "I recall a trail that leads through this portion of the Drops. Why are we not on it?" she asked.

Two Elks stared for a few moments and then climbed down next to her. "Trail dangerous. Watched. This way is safe."

Gaidel considered what she knew about the Drops. It was not uncommon for Two Elks' people to test their young braves by sending them into the Drops in small raiding parties. The very practice that led to the hostile relationship between their two peoples and why she knew it was not a good idea for her to be going there now with her new shieldwarden.

Why Mother Brambles had taken her out of the Cradle for her training was still a mystery to her. Why she had been bonded to a Nordlah Plains Barbarian an even greater one. She was the only Redwood Druid she had ever heard of to be bonded to a plainsman.

She motioned for him to continue. What was done was done. She was a Daughter of the All Mother and Two Elks was bonded to her. Those who did not accept that would find out soon enough how little she cared what they thought. Two Elks continued to stare. She glared at him until he turned back around and continued climbing. With his long reach and honed muscles, he made short work of the remaining climb.

When Gaidel reached the top of the ravine, Two Elks was moving towards her with shield and axe in hand, his face hard. "Come Daughter, I have found something."

"Call me Gaidel," she said. There was something about the way he said her honorific that irritated her.

She followed behind him for only a short distance. She smelled his find before she saw it. The grizzled remains of two bodies, cradlers by the looks of their clothes, lay mangled on the forest floor.

Gaidel swallowed down bile and brought her staff before her defensively, studying the woods.

"Day only. Less maybe. They are gone now," Two Elks said.

Gaidel lowered her staff and studied the faces of the two men, hoping she didn't know them. They had not been fed upon, she noted, though they had been savaged well beyond what it would have taken to kill them. She didn't recognize them, but if they were in the Drops, then they were most likely from Redwood village and her father surely would. Gaidel had to know what happened.

Closing her eyes, she breathed in deeply, clearing her mind of thought. She opened her senses. She willed herself to become one with the song and felt the essence of herself spread out and meld with everything around her.

At once the song of the All Mother poured in, filling her like an empty vessel. A song only a daughter could hear, feel, and taste. She sensed more than saw Two Elks protecting her as she swayed with the rhythm. She could feel the song flowing through her. Somewhere in the distance, she could hear herself singing.

Now she could feel the tiny feet of the ants as they thundered across her flesh, carrying their recently found boon down their tunnels deep within her. She was becoming lost within the song, forgetting who she was. She had to concentrate. Remember why she was here. She could feel her roots and the bark on her flesh. She listened to the song as it flowed past her and resisted the urge to be swept up in it.

If she was going to see what happened, she was going to have to sing against the flow of time. It felt like fighting upstream against a raging current. A current that pulled at her inner being. It would be so natural to give in and flow away with it.

She had to concentrate. She knew she was only strong enough to sing against the song for a short time, but if the attack had happened today, she would not have to go far to see what happened.

After a few moments Gaidel opened her eyes and leaned against the staff to keep her balance. She was always disoriented after leaving the song. When she regained her senses she motioned to Two Elks.

"Come, we need to bury them and sing their death. Then we hunt," she said.

9

The Cost of Discordance

T did not take them long to catch up with the vargan. Gaidel could hear the growls and grunts that made up their language before she saw them. She slid forward across the ground next to Two Elks. The sun warmed her shoulders as they crawled the last few feet, entering one of the many patches of sunlight filtering through the leafy canopy above.

The strong musty scent of the creatures irritated Gaidel's sense of smell, but Two Elks had taught her if the wind brought the smell of your prey to you, then it hid yours from them.

Peering over the lip of the ravine, the two watched as the vargan fought amongst themselves over their find. The half-eaten carcass of the elk might have been left behind by some other predator that was either sated from the kill or that the vargan had driven off.

The largest of them crouched over the carcass, baring jagged teeth in its wolf-like muzzle, daring the others to challenge its right to feed first. The others stalked around their leader, growling their displeasure.

There were only five of them, a small number, considering the vargan usually traveled in larger packs. Gaidel wondered why this group held so few and why it had risked raiding so close to the Cradle. Vargan were cunning, intelligent hunters and not known to take risks. The Cradle was home to humans and protected by the Redwood Druids. This small pack had chosen to hunt within the Cradle's boundaries and killed two of its people. Gaidel could still hear the discordant song the trees had sung where she and Two Elks found the bodies. From the trees she had learned the foresters had not provoked the vargan and confirmed the bodies had not been fed upon. To kill for food or in self-defense would have at least meant the vargan were living by the All Mother's laws, but this pack had done neither. They had killed the two men for the pleasure of it. She could not let that stand.

Gaidel and Two Elks rose up from the foliage as one, the bond they shared as druid and shieldwarden communicating intentions quicker than words. The vargan fell silent below them, ears twitching to locate the sound. Two Elks pulled the shield from his back in a practiced movement and slammed his stone axe against it, roaring a challenge.

Closing her eyes, Gaidel breathed in deeply and cleared her mind of all thought. She began to sing. Reality faded from view as she entered the song, flowing along with it. She could feel the sun's warmth on the tops of her many leaves, feeding her.

She lilted along the song, searching. There! She could sense them. The vargan's discordant beat fought against the surrounding rhythm. They were all young males. She growled with the rage she felt within them.

Concentrating, she beseeched the song to follow her rhythms and bring the powers of nature against those who would cause such discordance. The song ignored her as it thundered along. The winds continued to dance, laughing at her attempt to tame them. She was so young and her voice so small. She lowered her pitch and began singing to the trees in their own slow cadence.

At the sound of her song, the vargan attacked. They howled and barked as they fell from two legs to all four to climb out of the ravine.

Two Elks voiced his fury as they came, moving to keep himself between Gaidel and their attackers. Through the bond he sensed the song thundering deep within Gaidel and knew she was unable to defend herself when lost in the song.

The vargan leader reached Two Elks first and sprang out of the ravine, bringing its fangs and claws to bear. It never reached him. Its growl was cut off as a large branch swung down with bone crushing speed.

Two Elks raised his voice in thanks to the trees for answering Gaidel's call. Another branch swung through the charging pack forcing them to leap and dive to avoid the fate of their leader.

The vargan leader shook its head, trying to clear it. Bone jutted through torn flesh at its shoulder. Snarling through the pain, it rose only to meet the sharp head of a stone axe.

Two Elks felt the satisfying crunch as he brought the axe down. The vargan would not rise again. He immediately looked for another target. Of the remaining four, two lay on the ground unmoving. The other two jumped and tried to stay away from the swinging trees, leaves and debris swirling around them.

In unison, Gaidel's song and the trees' attack ceased. Gaidel opened her eyes and pulled her wooden staff from its leather bonds. She breathed deeply and concentrated to clear her mind and vision. She could still feel the vargan's pawed feet as they ran across her skin, felt their furred flesh give beneath her wooden limbs.

She could not ride the flows of the All Mother's song any longer without losing herself in them. She was only just raised as a druid. Though they had never truly fought together before, she somehow knew Two Elks was there protecting her until her senses returned.

The remaining two vargan snarled and focused their anger on Two Elks, glancing nervously at the now-motionless trees. They slowly stalked towards him, fanning out to present separate targets.

Two Elks seemed to wait as they flanked him. He must have sensed Gaidel had not quite freed herself of the song. He shook his axe to keep his enemies' attention. He did not have long to wait. They sprang towards him, one coming in low, the other high.

Two Elks raised his shield and pivoted, turning his shoulder to help absorb the impact. Letting the force of the vargan slamming into the shield spin him, he rolled his shield over his head and down towards the ground. The rotation brought his axe up in a low sweeping arc. The axe bit deep into the neck and shoulder of the low charging vargan, throwing it back in a spray of blood. Continuing the motion, Two Elks drove the other vargan, still against his shield, hard into the ground, allowing the momentum to carry him over, slamming his full weight into the now-pinned creature.

Gaidel stepped forward and brought her staff down one, two, three times on the creature's muzzle before it stopped struggling.

Two Elks rose, unsheathing his deer-bone knife, and went to be sure the others would not rise again.

Her first real battle and against five vargan no less. It had all happened so fast. Her hands were visibly shaking. Gaidel took a deep breath and suddenly felt like crying. It felt like she was just now remembering to breathe.

Two Elks returned, carrying a number of furred ears still dripping blood. Gaidel drew back in revulsion as he made to hand her two.

"What are you doing?" she said.

He motioned the grisly prize towards her again. "Good kills. These are yours."

"I don't want those!" she said.

Two Elks shrugged and started sorting through his pack for something to hold his new trophies.

"Young males forced to leave pack," Two Elks said as he set about his task. "Leader killed men to show strength." He glanced up at her. "You fought good." He seemed to think for a moment before adding, "Gaidel."

Gaidel started to reply that of course she did and the word he should use was 'well', but found herself just nodding.

"Hurry," Two Elks said as he stood and took off in a slow run. "Drops too dangerous come dark."

Gaidel took one last look at the scene and then hurried to catch up. If they could at least sight the South Falls before it was too dark to travel, they should be safe. In the morning, they would make their way up the cliffs into the Redwood proper. Redwood village was only a short distance from the falls. She would be home.

10

Redwood Village

ARGAS leaned lazily against the thick trunk of the redwood and stared out through its branches. He hated guard duty. His bow and spear leaned against the wooden palisade a short distance away. He knew he was supposed to keep his weapons closer and his bow slung, but he had just won that bow not a week before playing at dice and he would kiss the Hungerer's backside before he was going to leave it slung when he wasn't about to use it.

"Good way to ruin a bow", his paps had always said. He could brace his bow faster than anyone else in Redwood village he would be willing to wager twice.

Hargas glanced down the worn wooden planks of the wall-walk running along the palisade to make sure the guard sergeant wasn't coming. That old coot took his duties way too seriously.

Hargas stretched and walked along the palisade to get the blood flowing. He watched those below going about their business. He didn't see much traffic going or coming out of the Lady's Grace. He had been having a good bit of luck at the dice and had his eye on that metal blade of Torber's. He had almost gotten him to ante the blade up last night.

"Lady's Grace, my hairy backside," he muttered to himself and spat off the wall-walk. He watched the spittle drop onto one of the thatched roofs that ran along the inside of the palisade.

The inn used to be called the Three Arrows before Orson's daughter was chosen by the druids a couple of years back. It was a name Hargas preferred. Though the name had changed, the patrons had not. It was still the best place to go for a good game of dice and a Rock Stout. Even the new wooden sign of a druid reaching up with arms outstretched to the sky hadn't stopped the locals from calling it the Three Arrows.

By Daomur's beard, if it wasn't Orson's daughter herself.

Hargas saw the half-shaved head and blue curving tattoos that marked the druid walking on the high street below him. The largest plainsman Hargas had ever laid eyes on walked next to her, carrying the shield of a shieldwarden over his shoulder. It looked like a child's toy on him.

50

Hargas spat again and chuckled. Choosing a plainsman as a shieldwarden was daft enough, bringing him back to Redwood with her even more so. Hargas already saw heads turning and dark stares following the duo. The plainsmen were not liked. Maybe some of those uplanders would look past it, since he was a shieldwarden and all, but the folk of Redwood village were not uplanders. A man had to be good with the bow and spear in the Redwood, even better in the Drops where the best hunting was. Of course, they were used as much for protection against the raiding plainsmen as for hunting.

Hargas forgot about his guard duties and found a seat on the wall-walk to better see the front of the Lady's Grace. Guard duty was not going to continue to be boring, he would wager.

"My girl!" Orson called. He came from around the bar on the far side of the common room of the Lady's Grace.

Gaidel smiled at the man who had found her in the woods all those years ago and took her in as his daughter. She had only been away for two years, but his already portly belly had grown. She noted the healthy head of curly hair he had always been so proud of was now more gray than brown.

"Hello, Father," Gaidel said. She bowed and turned her palms upward.

"There will be none of that foolishness here girl," Orson said. He closed the distance between them, arms outstretched.

Two Elks started to step forward, but a tilt of the head from Gaidel stopped him. He tried to slow her father's advance, but Orson scooped her up in a loving hug.

"I have missed you, my girl. Let me look at you." He held her at arm's length and took the whole of her in. "I knew you were going to have to shave off those lovely red curls of yours, but what have you been eating? You are as thin as a Southfalls stork!" He gripped her arms and grinned. "Stronger though, if these muscles of yours have anything to say."

Gaidel let the Three Arrows pass over her like a warm breeze. The place had been her home until her coming of age. She felt that breeze carrying away the experiences of the past two years.

Long tables and benches of stained and well-worn redwood filled every available space. Only the entryway and the area around the central circular stone hearth were spared. She used to hide under those protective tables and tease the very same hunters and foresters she would later serve when she was older. The door to her father's private back rooms was open. She glanced at the stairway leading up to the second floor and the open room, where guests could rent a spot on the floor.

Her father followed her gaze and smiled wider. "Your room is just as you left it. I was hoping the festival was going to bring you back to me. Tell me you're staying longer than just one night?"

Gaidel smiled and gave him another hug. "Sorry, Da. Just for the night. We need to make for Lakeside and the festival. Mother Brambles will attend and has sent for me."

Orson seemed to notice Two Elks for the first time, sized him up, and found him wanting. Her father was the kindest man she had ever known. He had always been gentle and patient with her, but as an innkeeper he had to deal with all sorts and in a village like Redwood, those sorts could be pretty rough. He had developed a certain way of looking through a person; a turn of the head, a straightness to the mouth, that told a person he was not to be trifled with. He used that look on Two Elks now.

"A plainsman as your shieldwarden? The All Mother protect you, Dellie Girl."

Gaidel reddened at her father's childhood name for her. "Da, please."

"This one sleep upstairs," Orson said.

Two Elks, whose head had not cleared the lintel when they entered, looked down at him. "Daughter Gaidel sleeps where Two Elks can protect," Two Elks said. He crossed his thick arms over his chest to add to the sincerity of the statement.

Gaidel tried to contain her smile when she saw Orson's face change shades. She had seen him scrap with some of the meanest men in the Redwood, but thought he had met his match in Two Elks. At least ten years older than her, the shieldwarden was in his prime.

The scratching of nearby benches and the smack of cudgels being tested against hands told Gaidel her father would have help from his regulars, but Gaidel still feared Two Elks might hurt someone. The Three Arrows would consider a night unfulfilled if some mishap or insult didn't result in an offering of a tooth, or blood from a split lip or broken nose. But Two Elks had grown up on the Nordlah Plains and mishaps and insults usually resulted in deaths.

Gaidel reached up slowly and placed her hand on Two Elks' crossed arms. He didn't seem to notice any trouble and still stared matter-of-factly at the blustering innkeeper.

"Two Elks can sleep outside my door, Father," Gaidel said.

"Your locked door?" Orson said, still sizing up Two Elks for a beating.

"Of course, Da," Gaidel said. She bowed her head, holding her palms upward.

Orson sighed, patting her hands. "Stop that now. It's alright boys." He motioned the two towards a table near the hearth. The handful of men who had stood, ready to support the beating of the plainsman, hung their cudgels back on their belts and settled into the benches, with sighs of disappointment.

Gaidel knew there would be trouble if Two Elks remained in the common room for any length of time. Already news of the arrival of a plainsmen barbarian would have traveled through the village.

"Da, might we take our food and drink in the back rooms?" Her tone caused Orson to glance around.

"Nothing's gonna happen in the Lady's Grace what I don't let happen," Orson said this louder than was necessary.

"Even so, Father," Gaidel said in the voice she always used with him to get her way. She succeeded as he finally nodded.

"I also bring sad news. We found the bodies of two woodsmen in the Drops yesterday," Gaidel said.

"What happened?" Orson asked.

"It was the vargan," Gaidel said.

"Vargan hunting the Drops? Are you sure, Honored Daughter?" one of the closer patrons, who had obviously been listening in, asked.

"Yes, we hunted them down and punished them for what they had done," Gaidel confirmed.

Orson looked at the two of them as if for the first time and nodded, giving Gaidel another firm squeeze. "I'm sure you did, Girl." Orson thought for a moment or two. "Could be Tyber and his boy. We will send a party down. Tell us where to find them."

The stiffness in Gaidel's neck and shoulders slowly abated as she and Two Elks took their meal seated upon casks in the back room of the Three Arrows. She was home. Orson had even prepared her favorite dish, dove stuffed with garlic and mushrooms. He had insisted on cooking it for her. The familiar pangs of regret over leaving him returned.

55

His wife had died trying to give birth to his first child. Orson might have remarried, but had found a very young Gaidel hidden in the rotted-out nook of an old tree. She did not remember her family, but was told they had been foresters. They had fallen victim to a vargan raiding party somewhere in the Drops.

Orson had recounted the details of the day he'd found her. He was part of the group who had joined with the fangs to track the raiding party down. None of the men could coax her out of her hiding place. She had only come out when Orson had sung a song his Mattie used to sing while she cooked. The young Gaidel and her adopted father had been inseparable from that day until her Choosing. If it had not been for the pride on his face that day, she wouldn't have left him to become a druid.

But the inn kept him busy and he didn't seem to need a wife or a helper to keep it running. He seemed to have a wife in the Three Arrows, in every way that mattered to him. At least, that was the truth Gaidel convinced herself of.

"This was," Two Elks searched for the word, "home?"

Gaidel nodded and looked around the store room that doubled as Orson's room. She motioned to the small room beyond. "That was, or is, my room."

Two Elks downed the last of his drink and wiped his mouth on his bare forearm. He took another look around and shook his head. "You are from strange people, these Gwa A'Chooks."

The dwellings of the Cradle were still foreign to him. His people moved constantly across the plains, following the herds of giant tufters. His people built their whole society around those massive creatures. Their homes were made from their furs and long tusks. Almost all of their men were what the people of the Cradle considered fangs, protectors and followers of the way of the druids.

Two Elks' people thought of the cradlers as 'Gwa A'Chooks'. Her understanding of the plainsmen's tongue was not very good, but she thought it translated literally to 'spoiled animal of the dwarfs', or simply, 'dwarf's pets'.

Gaidel knew her people were strong and proud. A people who had found balance with Mother Allwyn and her children here in the Cradle of the Gods, just as the Nordlah Barbarians had found a balance with her in the plains. Life was not a stone, to be cut and carved to one's liking, but was an eternal song one had to join to find harmony.

Gaidel smiled warmly at her protector.

"As are we all."

11

The Three Arrows

ARGAS sat in the Three Arrows and steamed. He had waited on the wall-walk for a fight to break out in the inn until the Guard Sergeant had found him and added another shift to his time. He was going to give the old coot a piece of his mind, but finally had to admit it would only result in him getting more time added and probably a good thrashing to boot.

In Hargas' mind, the blame lay squarely on the shoulders of the plainsman. It was obviously his fault for distracting him from his duties.

Hargas had gone and found Torber, and his younger brother Seth, as soon as he had gotten off duty. He knew both of them loved a good fight and had more reason than most for disliking the plains-men. Their father had died in one of their raids into the Drops many years back.

The three now sat at their regular bench throwing dice. Torber still hadn't anted up that steel blade of his, but the night was young.

Torber was swirling the bones around in the leather cup. Hargas kept glancing at the closed door leading to the back, wondering when the plainsman was going to show his face. He hardly noticed when Torber slammed the cup down and hollered. He had yet another match. That was the third one in a row. By Daomur's beard, the fool had found his luck tonight.

"Ante up, I'm going for four," Torber said. He reached over and scooped up the dice.

"I'll take that wager," Hargas said, pushing four more stone arrowheads and some nice fletchings he had made earlier that morning into the already considerable pile.

Seth squinted at the ante and looked at his remaining pile. He only had a bow string and a stone knife left.

Hargas glared at him. "Well?"

"Naw, his luck is too good. I'm outta this one," Seth said. He leaned back and made a show of fishing the last dregs out of his mug. If he was waiting for Hargas to buy the next round, he was sadly mistaken.

"Looks like you and me, Harg. Seems only fair luck is on my side since you promised me a brawl that never happened," Torber said.

Hargas motioned towards Torber's belt. "Then put your blade in if luck is with you, braggart!"

Torber reached down to touch his prize possession defensively and shook his head. "Pot aint big enough for a metal blade, Hargas. It's going to take more than what you got on ya."

Hargas shook his head and spat on the floor. Nothing was working out right today. *Stinking plainsmen,* Hargas thought.

Just then, the plainsman walked out of the rear door.

Torber slammed the cup down, lifting it slowly just as the plainsman passed behind him. Hargas saw the fourth match. It was time to make his own luck.

He reached out under the table with his foot and shoved against the top of the bench Seth and Torber relaxed on. The bench tipped back, taking the surprised men with it. Torber swung his arms wildly trying to catch his balance, failed, and tumbled back into the barbarian, who deftly caught him before he could fully fall, but not before Torber's flailing legs upset the table, spilling its contents.

"Oi!" Torber yelled at Hargas, the tumbling dice, and the barbarian with equal outrage.

Seth was not as fortunate as Torber and didn't have anyone to break his fall. He tumbled to the floor.

Now we're getting somewhere, Hargas thought. He jumped up on his bench and dove across the table. "Damn savage! Get your hands off my friend!"

Two Elks had just wanted some more of the dark drink. The little daughter had retired early and he had spent the better part of the evening sitting on a barrel in front of her door. Her father had poked his head into the storeroom numerous times to make sure he remained on the right side of her door.

Two Elks shook his head. What did he think was going to happen? He was her shieldwarden. He was sworn to protect her. He thought of her more as a younger sister than anything else. Even if he had wanted to take her to his tent, he would have to make the proper offerings to her father first and get the blessings from the tribal mothers.

Two Elks would never admit to himself the laughing and drinking out in the common room had piqued his curiosity. He was just going out there to refill his mug and then return to his duty.

He saw the fat one shove the bench as he passed. He tried to catch both of the falling men, but only managed to catch the one. He didn't understand what the scrawny one he had caught was yelling about, but it didn't really matter. The fat one was coming over the table at him.

Gaidel had tried to tell him the differences between their people's ways. He knew these men wanted to challenge him. He was fine with that, welcomed it even. He didn't have the gifts he would have to offer their women for their loss, so he knew he shouldn't kill them. It was a mark on his honor to allow them to live, but he had to accompany the little daughter to these dwarf pet's festival and he was sure she wouldn't understand.

The punch that caught the fat one in the face landed soundly. Two Elks was surprised that was all it took to drop him. The one he was holding up with the other hand reached back and grabbed at him. He shrugged and let go. As soon as the skinny cradler lost his balance again, he forgot about trying to grab Two Elks and fell to the floor. The ugly one with the crooked teeth who had fallen with the bench was starting to rise.

Two Elks reached down and grabbed them both by their hair. It was greasy and his fingers almost slipped through. He tightened his grip and heaved them up. He gave them a good shake and then brought their heads together soundly. Not enough to kill them, but enough to end this quickly. He released his grip and the two crumpled in a heap.

The inn was silent. Two Elks looked for the next attack, but saw only stunned expressions. Was the challenge over? None of his tribe's seasonal camps were near the Drops, but if this was all the fight the cradlers had in them, it was no wonder the other tribes' young males went against them for sport. Gaidel's father stood near the central hearth. He hastily closed his open mouth when Two Elks met his gaze.

Two Elks reached down and picked up his mug. Walking over to the innkeeper, he held it out.

"More dark drink, Father of Daughter Gaidel. If it please you," he said.

He thought he had said it correctly and with proper respect. The man took the cup and filled it. All without saying a word. Two Elks took the cup and nodded his thanks. He walked through the quiet room, stepping over the three unconscious challengers. None of the patrons had yet to move as he closed the storeroom door.

Crazy cradlers.

12

Between a Rock and a Dark Place

HILE grazed his father's flock in the lowest fields of Upper Vale, under the protective shadow of the Horn. He tied his woolen coat around his waist and enjoyed the occasional warmer breezes that held the promise of the summer to come.

Life in Last Hamlet had returned to normal after the celebration and carried on much as it always had. Ghile already missed his Uncle Toren, who had returned to his patrols in the wilds surrounding the Cradle. He was probably already in the middle of his next great adventure. Ghile stifled a yawn with the back of his hand.

He watched one of the ewe's drift away from the flock and called for Ast and Cuz to round her up.

He would do it himself, but his arms were still tired from helping his mother and the other women sort the fleeces this morning. He didn't want to admit he was just being lazy.

The two Valehounds yawned, ignored him, and continued to lounge in the thick grass. He wasn't the only one being lazy. "Thanks for the help you two," he said. Ghile headed off the sheep and used the blunt end of his spear to marshal her back towards the others. Once he had her back he returned to leaning on his spear and looked about the Vale.

The Horn dominated the view and he followed the paths that crisscrossed its surface and the darker areas that marked caves with his eyes. Uncle Toren told him some went deep into the mountain. The people of the Cradle avoided the Horn. There were too many dangers that could befall the curious. Not even the mountain goats common to Upper Vale ventured on its pockmarked stones. It was said that humans had once lived in those caves and the ruins at the Horn's southern base. The tumble of worked stones the locals just referred to as the 'Ruins' was even more shunned than the Horn itself.

The ruins were older than anyone really knew and since all humans had been told the histories and their race's subsequent fall from the grace of the gods, anything that would remind them of that time was best avoided. Only the dwarfs were allowed to work the stone and build with it now. Most knew the humans of the past had practiced the art, but after the Great Purge, humans were forbidden many things to prevent them from making the same mistakes – stonework among them.

So, Ghile was surprised to see someone near the ruins. He wondered who would be foolish enough to venture near them. The man had a swaggering gait and long dark hair. Ghile shook his head when he recognized Riff. He watched Riff scout along the stones, then, seeming to find the entrance he wanted, disappear into its depths.

Ghile continued to stare after Riff. He was far enough away that he doubted Riff had seen him, if it even was him. Maybe this was where Riff found the metals he worked. But like anyplace not frequented by humans or patrolled by the fangs, there was no telling what might have made its home in there. It would take more than the lure of metals to inspire Ghile to venture into those black tunnels.

Ghile imagined what he would do if they never heard from Riff again. He saw himself standing before his father's hearth, telling the story of how the ruins had swallowed the young apprentice, his clansmen listening, eyes wide and mouths agape.

Something thudded onto the ground near Ghile, surprising him, and making him yelp. He turned to the sound of guffawing, face already reddening from embarrassment.

"Did you see him jump, Gar?" Bralf said, already searching for another stone.

"Ast! Cuz! Watch 'em," Ghile shouted. He had seen the two hounds rise up menacingly when his father had given them the same command.

They simply stared at him with blank expressions.
Stubborn hounds.

"Watch them!" Gar mimicked in a high voice. This set Bralf into more fits of laughter.

What were they doing down here? Probably dodging their responsibilities if Ghile didn't miss his guess.

"Looks like your dogs pay you as much heed as everyone else, Weed." Gar had a way of drawing out the word 'weed' in a way that grated along the inside of Ghile's ears.

With that, Gar closed one eye, took aim, and let fly. Ghile saw the rock zipping towards him and tried to jump aside. But, as always, his body did not respond to his commands fast enough and he barely turned to avoid catching the stone in his chest, instead thudding painfully against his shoulder.

He stumbled from the white hot pain of the blow as much as from the awkward position he found himself in and fell solidly to the ground.

Ghile remembered when Adon had protected him from the likes of Gar and Bralf. But since his culling, they had made it their sole purpose in life to torture the Clan Leader's last remaining clumsy son. Ghile thought of threatening to tell his father, but bit back the words. No matter what happened he would not use his father for protection.

He took a deep breath and decided to take a stand. The boys continued laughing. The sound of Bralf saying, "Here, try this one," changed Ghile's mind and set him into motion. He scrambled to his feet and fled. He heard the whistling of the rock slicing through the air, right before it struck him just above his ankle. Again he went down in a tumble of arms and legs, accompanied by more laughing.

Riff! Riff would help him and teach them a lesson. He scrambled to his feet and ran as fast as he could towards the ruins.

"Run, Weed!" Gar called behind him.

Ghile chanced a quick turn and saw they were in fast pursuit. Stones thudded near him as he ran in sharp angles trying to present a harder target. He ran as fast as he could, trying to avoid the jagged stones that jutted out of the thick grass.

The Ruins loomed larger at his approach and he tried to remember which of the many openings Riff had entered. Ghile didn't want to go in. Maybe taking the beating he was sure to get at the hands of Gar and Bralf would be better than what he might encounter in those dark passages? A rock barely missed his head. There was nothing for it now. He plunged into the nearest tunnel and was swallowed by darkness.

13

The Ruins

 "ɪꜰꜰ!" Ghile called again.

He called down another black tunnel that branched off the main corridor, then listened for a response.

Nothing.

He took a deep breath and darted to the next beam of light filtering through one of the many cracks in the ceiling. He pressed himself against the worn stone wall when he was near the light, but stayed just to the side of it. The darkness pushed in on him and made it difficult to breathe, but he had made the mistake of seeking solace in the first shaft of light he had seen. The bruises on his shins and arms still stung from everything he had run into or tripped over until his eyes had adjusted again.

He would have been content to just hide near the doorway he had originally dove through, but Gar and

Bralf had only been deterred by the ruins for a moment before following. Ghile warned them that the sorcerer's apprentice was here with him, but they ignored him; Gar promising him a worse beating for fleeing into the desolate place. He had no choice but to flee further in.

"Riff, where are you?" Ghile called down the next tunnel as loud as he dared. He thought he had lost Gar and Bralf, but didn't want to take any chances.

His feet kicked up dust where the ground was dry between the cracks in the ceiling, where rivulets of water seeped down into pools of mud. His fingers traced the straight indentations between the worked stones, feeling the moss and bracken that clung to life between them.

He saw another shaft of light ahead. The corridor opened into an angled room. The light stabbed in through the ceiling revealing three more tunnels leading off in opposite directions.

Ghile forced a swallow and took a moment to catch his breath. Where to go now? He was already hopelessly lost. Maybe he would hear Riff and it would help him decide which tunnel to take. He held his breath and listened. Only silence greeted him. Well, at least he didn't hear Gar and Bralf. They had hopefully given up and gone to find someone else to torment.

He slid down along the wall and pulled his knees close to his chest, wrapping them with his arms. He was in a fine mess now. He thought about the flock he had left grazing on the hillside. He hoped Ast and

Cuz would take his absence as reason enough to mind the flock, but doubted it.

Ghile sat there for a short while, listening to the wind blow outside and watched the dust motes float in and out of the light. If he didn't get out of here soon, the sun would go down and the light with it. The idea of being lost in the ruins in the dark caused his throat to start closing again. He took in deep steadying breaths.

A sudden glint on the ground caught his eye. His fear forgotten, he moved his head back and forth 'til he saw the flash again. There it was. Since entering, he had seen nothing in the stone tunnels and rooms. He slid forward for a closer look.

He brushed the crusted dirt back from where he had seen the glint. A hard surface resisted his probing fingers. Peering at it closely, he realized it wasn't stone. It was smooth and worked. Metal? He began clearing more dirt away. After a short time, he had a circular outline uncovered. He tried to pry it loose. One side of the ring reluctantly came up with a high pitched squeak. It was a handle. A metal handle? Only dwarves could afford to use metal to make anything as mundane as a handle. But these were not dwarven ruins. These were from before the gods had punished man. Had his people once been so rich as to have handles made of metal like the dwarves? Maybe this was why Riff had come here?

So, sorcerers had their ways, did they?

Ghile wiped his hands on his tunic and got a better grip on the handle. Taking a deep breath, he gave a measured pull. He was excited when he felt the handle give, but was shocked to see a large square portion of the floor come up with it.

The square stone fell back to the floor as Ghile let go. He could make out the outline of the square on the floor. He got another firm grasp on the handle and pulled. The stone panel resisted at first, but then came up and all the way over.

The shaft of light that had revealed the first glint of the handle now streamed into the opening, invitingly dancing down a set of stairs. He cautiously inched forward and peered into what looked like a small room. He counted a dozen steps. The light shining in from above allowed Ghile to make out debris that looked like the remains of an old table and benches that had given under the weight of years. He didn't know if it was greed or curiosity that lent him the strength to venture slowly down the stairs. There was probably more metal down there.

At the base of the stairs, Ghile's hunt for metal was forgotten when he saw the silhouette of a man standing just out of the light. Ghile yelped and turned to flee up the stairs. He felt his foot settle halfway between the first and second step before slipping out from under him. He fell hard against the steps and spun onto his back to see what the man was going to do. The man had not moved. In fact, he was perfectly still. Ghile massaged the pain in his hands, not daring to take his eyes off the still figure; he didn't even blink.

The figure stood frozen. Ghile wished he had an everflame torch. The light was not enough to make out details. He cautiously approached the figure, letting his eyes adjust. It was only a statue of a man. He had seen dwarf statues before, but never a statue of a human. The man stood tall and straight, his head tilted slightly up, giving him a conceited air.

It was then that Ghile noted the circular design on the man. A series of mounds formed a strange spiral shape in the middle of his chest. Ghile reached tentatively and began to run his fingers along the pattern. When his fingers brushed the first mound they held fast. Ghile tried pulling his hand back, but his fingers wouldn't come loose. Quickly, he braced his other hand against the statues chest to give him leverage – when it too stuck fast.

Ghile panicked.

He tried to shake himself free, but the statue was unmovable. He could feel his hands getting warmer. What was happening? Had he stumbled upon a statue of an ancient sorcerer and a trap he had left to punish thieves? Was this a burial tomb? He began to scream for help. He didn't care who heard him now. He would thank his ancestors if Gar and Bralf appeared in the portal above him, laughing at his misfortune.

"Riff! Help me!"

His hands were hot. He heard a low hum, like in the hives the beekeeper kept. The humming was coming from the statue. The statue began to glow from within. Every part of Ghile told him to flee, to get as far away from this place as he could. The statue was glowing too bright to look at and the hum now thundered in his ears. He screamed until his voice gave out.

Both hands were flat against the statue now. The heat transformed into intense pain in his left hand, a slicing pain along his palm. All his attention turned there as he tried to see what was cutting him, but his palm was pressed firmly against the statue and the light was blinding.

The pain was moving away from his palm and along the back of his hand. He struggled to keep his eyes open against the light. Tears streamed down his cheeks. A circular mound moved just under his skin, the shape and size the same as one of the stones in the statue's chest. Inch by agonizing inch the pain slid along the back of his hand and over his wrist. He wasn't sure if he was screaming anymore, but he thought he was.

He squeezed his eyes tight, though he could still see the shape of the statue burned into his vision. The searing pain had reached his shoulder. His mouth was dry and he felt cold sweat on his face. He couldn't feel his legs. The light was drifting away down tunnels now, taking the pain with it. He felt himself falling to the floor. He kept on falling. Falling down until all he felt was the burning now deep in his chest.

Then he felt nothing.

14

The Dreaming

" AKE up, little brother."

Ghile jolted up at the sound of his brother's voice.

"Adon?"

Ghile looked around. Where was he? Gravel shifted under him. He was on a tree-lined lake shore. He couldn't tell exactly what time it was. He stood up.

The sun was well into the sky, but it wasn't in the right place. Noon maybe? He heard birdsong. It was much warmer than it should be for spring in the Cradle. This was no part of the Cradle he had ever seen before. He wondered if he had fallen asleep in his bed. Ghile looked around, confused.

He looked for Adon. His voice was so clear. Had he dreamt it? Was he still dreaming?

"Yes and no," Adon replied.

Ghile spun and fell backwards, then began scrambling back across the shifting pebbles.

Adon laughed and shook his head. "Still clumsy, I see."

Ghile tried to form words, but his mouth just opened and closed like a fish. "You. Where? How can you?" He finally managed to get out.

Adon sat down on the shore next to his brother. He picked up one of the smooth, worn stones and studied it a moment before sending it out, skipping across the lake. Ghile's eyes followed the stone. He could see the forest on the far side. The land rose up from the water to form a stony mountain wall around them like a bowl.

"Adon, you're dead."

"Yes, but here I am. Isn't it beautiful here?"

"I don't understand," Ghile said.

"Let's just say you are different now and part of that difference allows you to come to this place when you sleep. You are dreaming. But this place, you and me, we are not part of the dream. We are very much real."

Ghile thought about this. He took in the sky and the forest behind him. He reached down and picked up one of the stones. He could feel its damp coolness, the weight of it. He squeezed and held it tight, like an anchor, afraid to let go.

"Why?" Ghile said.

"So you can learn. Ghile, I'm very excited for you. You have been chosen for something so very important. There are secrets our people once knew that have been taken from us. I have been given permission to share them with you again. To teach them to you."

"Why?"

"Chance. Luck. Fate. Does it really matter? It's you."

Ghile stared. Adon brushed the hair from his face, just like he used to. The long thin nose, just like their father's. It was Adon, just as he remembered him. "I miss you, Adon. We all do."

Adon reached out and squeezed his arm. "I know, little brother, I know." Adon looked out over the lake, then closed his eyes and breathed in deeply. "I like it here. Now you can come visit me whenever you wish."

Ghile saw motion in the woods, just over Adon's shoulder. He watched as a shadow peeled away from the dark trunk of one of the trees. Something about the shadowy creature looked familiar. The shadow was tall and thin, but appeared smaller due to the way it moved. It was hunched over, wringing its hands together, unsure of itself. It seemed to make up its mind and sprang forward with a burst of speed, launching itself at Adon.

Ghile screamed out a warning too late. The creature had already closed the distance and was coming down towards Adon's back. Right before it struck Adon, it slammed into some unseen force. Adon turned quickly and with a thrusting motion of his arm sent the creature hurtling back into the woods.

His hand never made contact with the shadow creature.

The stone tumbled from Ghile's hand, forgotten.

"You are not wanted here, shadow! Be gone!" Adon yelled after the tumbling creature.

Ghile watched as the shadowy form stumbled to its feet and disappeared into the woods, wringing its hands as it went.

"What was that?" Ghile said, watching it flee.

"A pathetic creature that unfortunately, also inhabits this island." Adon turned to Ghile, his face stern, "Do not trust it, Ghile. It has tried to lure me into traps many times. You must never try to speak to it or follow it. It means me, and now you, ill."

Ghile nodded. "Alright, I will remember." He couldn't shake the feeling there was something familiar about the shadow. "Adon, how did you do that?"

Adon smiled, crossing his arms over his chest, "That is what I'm going to teach you."

15

Awakened

OOL wetness pressed against Ghile's forehead and cheeks. He could hear talking coming from somewhere far off. He recognized the voices as they drew nearer. He smelled smoke, earth, and warm wool.

Ghile opened his eyes and saw his mother kneeling on the floor beside him. When their eyes met, she pursed her lips to keep them from trembling, but it did not stop the tears racing down her cheeks. "He's awake, Ecrec!" she cried.

Ghile's father moved to kneel behind his mother. His face was stern, but Ghile could see relief in his eyes. "You had your mother worried near to death, boy. What were you doing in those ruins?"

Ghile started to answer. His throat felt as if he had spent the morning sweeping the house with his tongue.

"Not now, Ecrec," Elana said. "Here, Ghile. Drink this." She handed him a mug. The water slid down his throat and settled into his empty stomach. The water woke pangs of hunger which began kicking against Ghile's ribs. "I'm starving," Ghile said.

Light shone in his mother's eyes and she laid a hand on her husband's. "Blessings to the All Mother, he is hungry. I'll be right back."

"Thank you, Mother." Ghile watched her hurry over to their central hearth. He was home. Ghile rose to a sitting position, his sleeping mat warm beneath him. He could see daylight through the entryway into the roundhouse and the three windows had their single shutters raised outward, propped with sticks to let in the light and crisp spring air. "How did I get here, Father?"

Ecrec looked behind him at Elana, hurriedly preparing Ghile's meal. When he turned, his jaw muscles were clenched, his eyebrows pulled tightly together. "Riff carried you all the way from those ruins. Ghile, you know they are forbidden. Your duty was to the flock. You had no business in there."

"Riff? Where is he?" Ghile asked.

"What?" Ecrec seemed caught off guard by the question. "He and Master Almoriz are still here." Ecrec gestured to another part of the roundhouse at the packs and sleeping mats. "They have been at your side since Riff brought you back. But that is not important. I have no idea what you were thinking, boy. But you are not going to—"

"Ghile! Ghile!" Tia screamed from the doorway. His little sister ran across the room, her straw baby swinging in her hand as she came. She barely stopped in time to avoid running him over, instead bounding into his arms. "I'm so glad you're okay, Ghile! Were you eaten by a ghost?" she asked, her eyes wide with hope.

Ghile smiled, shaking his head.

Ecrec lifted Tia and set her in his lap. "Now, now flower, let your brother breathe. He has just now returned to us." He took in a breath to continue, but Elana returned, kneeling down and starting to spoon warm broth into Ghile's mouth. Ecrec exhaled, defeated. Ghile gave silent thanks for his mother's interruption.

"I can do that, Mother, thank you." Ghile took the bowl and spoon. Elana handed him some bread, then sat back, leaning against Ecrec.

Ghile looked at the three of them, leaning on each other, staring at him with concerned expressions. His family. He had the sudden urge to tell them about his dreams and Adon, but didn't.

One of the last things Adon had warned him against was talking with anyone about the dreams or his training. He had said people would not understand. People always feared what they did not understand and at best they would think him crazy.

"Well, look who is back amongst the living." Master Almoriz had just entered the roundhouse, followed closely by Riff.

Ghile smiled and started to set his food down to make a proper greeting.

"Now, now, young Ghile," Almoriz chided. "You need to regain your strength. You have been asleep for two days."

"Two days?" Ghile said in a whisper.

He had been training with Adon on the island for what seemed a week. Ghile had ample time to explore his new dream place. It was a forested island dotted with little clearings. The island was small enough to walk completely around in half a day. In its center, Adon had shown Ghile a huge oak tree as thick as a roundhouse and reaching incredibly high into the sky. Ghile could sit on one of its roots with his feet dangling far above the ground. This is where they had trained and rested. There was no need for shelter, the weather was warm and it had never rained. Ghile had felt safe there. He had never dreamt, never been hungry, but always woke up refreshed and eager to learn.

The island sat in the middle of a large mountain lake, the forested crags rising up on all sides beyond the lake's waters. Four separate waterfalls poured into the lake from four opposite sides. It was beautiful.

Adon said it was his home now and Ghile could come visit him whenever he slept. How could Ghile explain this to anyone? Adon was right, they would never believe him.

"Riff, thank you for coming to my aid," Ghile said.

Riff smiled. "I stumbled upon you laying in the middle of one of the ruin's rooms, unconscious. I could not wake you. You gave me quite a scare."

Ghile was confused. "In the middle of a room? What about the statue?"

Riff glanced at Almoriz before answering. "Statue? There was no statue, Ghile. Those ruins are naught but empty rooms and passages."

"No, there was a door in the ground with a huge metal handle. I opened it and found stairs leading down. A statue." They were all staring at him, Riff shaking his head.

"Riff was in those ruins gathering sources for me," Master Almoriz said. "Even though it is a place best left alone—"

"It is forbidden, Master Almoriz," Ecrec said.

"We have need that outweighs the dwarves' restrictions, and have found sources there in the past. But, it is a dark place with many uneven stones and crevasses. You had no business there and are lucky Riff found you."

Ghile didn't understand what was happening. Why did Riff not admit to finding him in the room with the glowing, humming statue? He resisted the urge to touch his chest. Everyone was looking at him with mixed expressions of confusion and sympathy. Everyone except Master Almoriz and his father. Their stares were intense, almost angry. Ghile felt himself getting upset, too. Something told him their shared look was caused from very different concerns. But, he also knew now was not the time to try and find out, so he changed the subject. "The flock?" Ghile asked.

"Luckily, Ast and Cuz tended them well," Ecrec said. "Though, the real question is, why you were in those ruins."

"Father. I am sorry. I saw Riff." He started to tell his father about Gar and Bralf, like so many times before, but feared the pitying look his father would give him. Before he could continue, Ecrec handed Tia to her mother and rose.

"Master Almoriz, as you can see, he is fine. It is time for you and your apprentice to be on your way."

"Ecrec, please," Elana began.

"No, Elana. Ghile would never have gone near those ruins. He knows his place. I do not want *him* filling his head with nonsense." Ecrec jabbed a finger towards Riff.

"Me?" Riff said. "How is this my fault? I brought him to you."

Everyone began speaking at once. Not to be out-done, Tia began crying.

Ghile had to get out. He made a pained face. "I need to go outside."

The others stopped and moved to let him up. He raced out into the welcomed open air. He could hear the others start again so he hurried away.

His relations greeted him with cheers and waves, or questions of, "Are you well?" He assured them all and made his way to the privies near the far palisade wall. As he went inside one of them, he quickly undid his tunic and lifted it above his head. It stank of old sweat.

He ran his fingers along his skin until they reached the center of his chest. There he felt the hard surface of a round stone just under his skin. He tried to move it in vain, discovering it was joined firmly to the bone. The skin around it was smooth and pink, not irritated in the least at this newest addition. His left palm was likewise unmarked.

Then it was not all a dream.

He turned and looked at the door. He closed it slowly and dropped the latch into place, without ever touching it.

16

Across the Mountains

 HE pack made good time through the mountain pass. The wind howled, whipping snow into a flurry, partially blinding Muk. The goblin buried his face into Bloody Maw's back for protection, but immediately regretted it. Bloody Maw stank of wet fur and greasy worg's musk.

His knees ached. The worg's back was too wide. He wondered if other goblins suffered like this when they rode the wolves his kind normally used as mounts. Bloody Maw was twice their size.

His mount was apparently oblivious to the snow-storm. Its powerful gait had not slowed for hours, jumping from one rocky outcropping to the next, only moving over snow when absolutely necessary. Muk had at first cursed at Bloody Maw for jumping from rock to rock and not taking a more direct path through the pass, but the mental images he saw in the worg's mind of them being swallowed by one of the many snow-filled crevasses curbed his tongue.

Muk tightened his grip and peered into the whiteness behind him. He could barely make out anything. Tilting his head, he could just hear the occasional sound of a heavy paw pounding against stone or compacting snow. The pack was doing its best to keep up, but Bloody Maw set a grueling pace.

As pack alpha, Bloody Maw was the largest and fiercest. He was also the hardest one to control, which was why Muk rode him. It was still easier to dominate their minds and control them when they were close. Though, he noted with more than a little bit of pride, it was becoming easier to control them from a distance.

In the beginning, they would drop from his control if they strayed too far, forcing him to reassert his will when they returned to the pack confused and angry. But he had all but full control of them now, all except Bloody Maw. He could feel Bloody Maw's thoughts scratching at the periphery of his mind, digging, probing, and looking for a weakness or flaw, anything to reassert control.

Muk could not allow it. He had no doubt of his fate if he let that happen. What Bloody Maw and his pack had done to Bulak was still deeply ingrained in his memory. Muk grinned, his tongue absently sliding over small pointed teeth, as he recalled becoming leader of the Dark Skulkers.

Muk had walked proudly into Bulak's lair. It was one of the few buildings in that portion of the deserted human city with any semblance of a roof. There were many entrances into the lair through the various cracks in the walls. Muk chose to walk through the central door, the one entrance reserved for the leader of the tribe. No other goblin was allowed to use that entrance, save Bulak.

The Goblin Leader sat upon his gathered treasures, his furred bodyguards around him. The wolves rose, sensing their master's displeasure, hackles rising, waiting for the command to rip Muk to pieces. The numerous goblins gathered in Bulak's lair went silent, eyes darting between the two. Muk knew they were waiting to see how their leader would respond to this insult. Some of the older warriors grinned wickedly. He knew they thought him good as dead. He was a mere gatherer in the tribe, not a warrior. He had no followers and owned no wolves to support any claim to lead.

Bulak did not rise. He simply pointed at Muk and laughed, the laughter of the others joining in. Muk growled and tightened his fists. They did not know he had changed. Muk was powerful now. They would find out soon enough.

Bulak leaned down and whispered to the eager wolves, never taking his eyes off Muk. Bulak's grin told Muk the old leader thought this young upstart was about to die. The wolves snarled and leaped forward, each one trying to be first to reach their prey.

Muk ignored them and looked about the lair. He watched other goblins as their eyes followed the charging wolves. Some stared at Muk in disbelief, wondering why he did not run. He ignored them all.

He concentrated and could sense the wolves' minds. It felt as if he could reach out and touch their thoughts. He could sense the thrill of the kill within them. They were close enough. He reached out with his mind and grabbed theirs. He shredded them. He pulled the scattered mental threads into him. Fed on them. The effect on the wolves was instantaneous. Some fell to the floor rolling in pain. Others jumped upwards, twisting as they tried to escape this unseen foe. Within moments they all lay crumpled before Muk, one still twitching. Without the mind, the body died.

He looked across the lair at Bulak. The goblin leader was no longer smiling. It was Muk's turn to smile. He raised his arms into the air for effect as he sent out the mental summons. The worg pack charged through the many openings as one. The surprise on Bulak's face was quickly replaced with fear. He called for his goblin guards to protect him.

Under Muk's mental control, Bloody Maw and the pack fell on Bulak and the few warriors of the tribe foolish enough to try and protect him. Many fled. All goblins feared worgs. All goblins but Muk.

He walked past the feasting worgs and settled on Bulak's treasures. Muk noted an old human shield he himself had gathered. They were all his now.

His memories of the days that followed were pleasant ones. His tribe grew as other goblin tribes heard the leader of the Dark Skulkers kept worgs as bodyguards. Under his leadership, the Dark Skulker's territory within the city grew. The wolves the other goblins used stood no chance against worgs. Muk had thought he would one day rule the entire city. Maybe even challenge the dwarves who patrolled the outskirts of the city on those flying creatures.

That was when the dream goblin had told him of another stone. One that would grant him even more power. The dream goblin told him where to find it. Muk would not be sated until he had it. Something had changed within him and he was no longer content to be leader of the Dark Skulkers, or every goblin tribe scattered amongst the ruined human city. He had changed since he found the stone in that human statue. He growled as he remembered the pain.

Muk risked letting go of Bloody Maw's fur to run his fingers over his chest. The stone was there, a hard mound just beneath the skin. He had tried to remove it initially. Nothing could be further from his mind now. He and the stone were one. Muk knew the stone brought the dreams and with the dreams came the dream goblin.

The dream goblin had taught him many things. He learned how to reach out and touch the minds of animals and force them to obey. That was just the beginning. He was even now learning how to reach into their minds and see how they did things. He was learning to take those thoughts as his own. He could run as fast as a wolf or climb the wall as well as the huge spiders who dwelled in the deeper part of the ruins. Smaller animals were too weak and died when he ripped skills from their small minds. How hard that had seemed at first. How trivial it was now. His stolen abilities never lasted long, but now it was much easier for him to take them.

He was jarred and almost thrown from Bloody Maw's back as the worg leaped over a large gap and landed awkwardly on the other side. Muk cursed and reached into Bloody Maw's mind, scolding him for the discomfort. "Be more careful!" He waited for the groveling and apologies he knew would come.

"Forgive, Master. The gap was wide," Bloody Maw responded in his deep, growling way.

Muk was pleased. He enjoyed the respect his power brought. But it was not enough, he reminded himself. He could not, try as he might, reach into the minds of the other goblins. It seemed only the minds of animals opened to him. But, the dream goblin promised him more power from the magic stone across the mountains.

The Dream goblin had shown him the stone and the one who carried it. How he hated the little human boy. How dare he use Muk's stone! He would find the boy and take his stone. The rest he would leave for Bloody Maw.

"Are you sure this pass will take us through the mountains, Bloody Maw?" Thinking of his prize was making him impatient.

Blood Maw's response echoed in his mind. "Yes, Master. The ugly mountain is not far."

He wished he could see through this thrice-cursed snow. If he could, he might see this ugly mountain for himself. He had been shown it in his dreams and seen it in Bloody Maw's thoughts, but those images were so hazy. If he had been standing, he would have begun jumping from foot to foot with impatience.

"Find the mountain and you will find the boy", the dream goblin had told him. Yes, Muk would find this human boy. He would find him and kill him.

17

There is More

 EVER trust them," Adon said.

Ghile relaxed on one of the many roots extending from the giant oak in the center of the island, his feet hanging over the side as he rested. Adon had decided to use the time to reinforce his views on the dwarves.

"I don't, Adon." Ghile had already told him this. He looked around to see if the shadow was making another attempt on them. The warm breeze was the only thing stirring. It appeared they would be left alone today.

Adon stood on the ground, a short distance below, watching him with concern. Ghile knew how Adon felt about the dwarves. Who could blame him? They had taken his life. If not for Ghile finding this magic stone, Adon would still be lost in the afterlife.

"Adon, are you sure you do not remember what happened? Where you were?" Ghile wanted to know what happened after you died.

Adon refused to talk of his culling and only had vague memories of his afterlife with the elders. This hadn't stopped Ghile from consistently returning to the subject whenever there was a lull in his training.

"I have already told you everything I remember, little brother," Adon said.

"I'm sorry, Adon. It is just all so incredible." Ghile motioned around him. "Look at this place. The things we can do. It works the same when I'm awake. It is incredible. And I can't tell anyone!" Ghile shouted to the forest.

Adon smiled at the outburst. "That's right little brother – no one. The dwarves will kill you if they find out. I still think going through with the manhood tests is foolish."

Ghile shook his head. "What am I to do, Adon? You know it is expected."

"Leave, Ghile. Pack up what you will need and leave."

"Where would I go? The Cradle is my life."

Adon shook his head. "Not anymore, Ghile. Things are different now. You are different now."

Ghile nodded. He saw the truth in Adon's words. He was different. He had always dreamed of leaving the Cradle and living a life of adventure. But now that he was on the cusp of this decision, he didn't know if he could. What about his family? How could he do that to his mother? What would his father think?

Would he think Ghile ran from the tests? Then there was the issue of the dwarves. Would they know?

The manhood tests were a tradition and a matter of honor for his people. Every girl of age for handfasting went to the festival. They all knew it was law that they attend the Rite of Attrition. It was just something you did for the good of all.

"Why did you teach me this, Adon? Why have you done this to me?" Ghile's throat got tighter and his eyes stung. He would not cry. He breathed in deep and swallowed. "I am so glad to see you, but I didn't ask for any of this."

Adon nodded. "I know." He walked up next to the large trunk and looked up at Ghile. "It is knowledge that has been lost for too long. You found me, remember?"

Ghile nodded and closed his eyes. "What's done is done."

Adon nodded, watching him. "So, you're going to leave?"

"No." Ghile shook his head. "I will not do that to our family. I will keep you and this place a secret. I will learn the lost knowledge of the old ones. But I will not leave our family."

Adon only stared at him, sorrow in his eyes.

"And I will take and pass my manhood tests and the Rite of Attrition," Ghile finished.

Adon shook his head, but apparently decided not to push the issue just then. "Fine, little brother."

Ghile slid off the root and let himself drop towards the ground. He concentrated on his feet and pushed his will through them. He pictured his will as a tangible force and willed it to flow from the bottoms of his feet. He could see it in his mind, pushing out and forming a thick shimmering plane.

He could feel his descent slowing as the force touched the ground first and was pressed together. He waved his hand to keep his balance as his momentum was slowed and had almost reached the ground when the pressure was too much and the force he had created by will alone snapped out of existence.

He dropped the last foot and absorbed the last of the momentum with his knees. He looked up at the top of the root and figured the drop was around twenty feet. He smiled at Adon.

Adon nodded approvingly. "Not bad."

Ghile laughed and feigned being insulted. "Not bad?"

Adon smirked. "Yes, not bad."

Suddenly a large rock came flying from Adon's hand as he shouted, "But can you do it quickly!"

Ghile only had a moment to respond, he focused his thoughts and raised his hand, forcing his will through it. He only needed a little force to deflect the stone, but what if he formed it like he did when he was trying to slow a fall? Just as the rock reached him, it slowed. In the past it had reflected off the force shield he would have created, but this time it just slowed as its momentum was taken in by the shield. When it had all but stopped, Ghile willed the force to push it away.

The rock hurled back towards Adon, whose eye widened as he brought his own hand in front of him and brought forward force to block the small projectile. He nodded approvingly. "Now that was not bad!"

Ghile smiled. This was so different than all the other training he had ever done. At this, he was a natural. He would love to have Gar and Bralf throw another stone at him now.

"Ghile?" Adon had closed the distance between them and Ghile noted a change in his demeanor.

"Yeah?" Ghile said.

"You are glad I'm here in this place, aren't you?"

"Of course, you know that. Why would you even ask?"

Just then, Ghile heard a twig snap behind him. He turned quickly and saw the shadow creature disappear into a thicket. It had been watching them again.

Ghile reached for his pouch. If he could just get a stone out in time.

"No, Ghile. Don't," Adon said loudly, reaching down and taking him by the hand.

Ghile was taken aback. Adon had told him not to trust the shadow creature and had used stones and even the magic to drive it away.

"Why not?" Ghile asked, removing his hand from his pouch and watching the creature slip deeper into the forest. Ghile wondered why Adon had spoken so loudly. He was right next to him.

Adon watched the creature leave and then removed his hand. He turned and started walking the other way.

"It was already leaving, I saw no need to attack it," Adon said.

"But you said it was dangerous and not to trust it. It has tried to attack you numerous times and has tried to lure me into the forest just as many." Ghile still didn't understand why the shadow creature attacked Adon openly, yet only ever tried to lure him deeper into the forest to attack him. He asked Adon.

Adon shrugged. "It knows I am the teacher and the greater threat, perhaps?"

"Why don't we just hunt it down and kill it?" Ghile asked. Ghile didn't understand why it was even here, if this was a place he had created. He definitely wouldn't have dreamed up a skulking monster to inhabit an island paradise.

Adon shook his head. "It would do no good, little brother. I have tried that when you were not with me and it just disappears. It is very adept at remaining hidden when it wants to."

Ghile finally shrugged. "Alright."

"Come, back to practice," Adon said.

18

A Heavy Burden

s this what death is like?" Ghile asked. He was leaning against the huge oak; the large patterns in the bark worked well when he needed a good scratch. The warm breeze and the silent forest along with the full day of training had done its work. His eyelids felt heavy. He could feel his breathing falling into that deep rhythmic pattern just before sleep.

Adon leaned against the trunk near him, looking up at the sky. "You are just going to keep asking, aren't you? Even though I said I don't really remember," Adon said. He took his hands from behind his head and crossed them over his chest.

Ghile shrugged and smiled a little. "You have to remember something. You know all these secrets from our ancestors. You had to speak with them."

"Listened to them," Adon interrupted. He was silent for a moment and then sighed, looking like he had finally resigned himself to something. "I listened to them. Ghile, the afterlife is not like this place. Here we are someplace. There is this island and on it a forest. It sits in the middle of this huge lake and the mountains rise up around it," Adon said.

Ghile nodded.

"But what lies beyond the mountains?"

Ghile thought about this and looked through the branches at the distant mountains. "I never really thought about it. More mountains, I guess."

"I'm not so sure. I think of this as an in-between place. I don't think we could any more leave this island and pass over those mountains than we could breathe the water in the lake. This place is real enough, don't get me wrong, but it is not anywhere on Allwyn."

Ghile considered this for a little while. "And when you die, you don't go somewhere like this?"

"No, you don't. It is like dreaming. It isn't unpleasant. It's nice. Like a nice dream. But like a dream, you are there, but not really. You see things, experiencing things from your life. But you are not *there*," Adon said, putting emphasis on the last word.

"Then how did you hear the elders?" Ghile understood dreaming well enough. He knew he was dreaming now. He ran his hand along the bark of the old oak. *So real*, he thought.

Adon had to consider that for a moment, "Well, imagine being in a field which is filled with other people. You are laying there in the grass with your eyes closed."

Ghile pictured himself there as Adon described it. He could see all the people spread out around him.

"Now imagine it is completely dark. No moon or stars to see by. Now everyone begins whispering about their lives."

Ghile imagined the scene and realized how confusing that would be. "It would sound like bees buzzing," he said.

Adon chuckled. "Yes, it did at first. But, you can eventually block out the ones you are not interested in and focus on the ones you are."

"Is it like that forever?" Ghile didn't know if he liked the sound of it. Being somewhere, but not really being there. Spending eternity listening to other people's memories of their lives. Having people listen to his. "Were you reliving your life? Were people listening to you?" Ghile asked.

"Of course. Though, you don't realize it at first. Keep in mind you are not just listening. Once you focus in on a specific memory, you see it like it's your dream. I could see doing that for a very long time. There are some ancient dreamers there, Ghile."

"Do you wish to go back?" Ghile wondered if he had done something wrong by bringing Adon here. Maybe that was where he was supposed to be, and now Ghile had trapped him in this in-between place forever.

"No," Adon said emphatically. "Ghile, you know what was missing there? What should have been there, but wasn't?"

Ghile leaned forward, focusing on Adon's features.

"Dwarves. Or any of the other races of Allwyn. There were only human dreamings. I don't think we are supposed to be there forever. I don't think that is the after-life. I think that place is where some of us go, ever since our god was banished."

"Banished? He was imprisoned, Adon. Daomur and Islmur defeated him in battle and imprisoned him beneath the mountain city of Daomount."

Adon shook his head. "His prison is not in Allwyn, though. Ghile, there are dreamers still there who remember the times of the Great Purge. When the dwarves and elves slaughtered entire cities of our people. I have seen some of those memories, Ghile. It was a horrible time."

Ghile swallowed and wondered what other things Adon had seen in the four years since his death at the hands of the dwarves.

"The All Mother, Allwyn, did awake and command the slaughter to stop. She didn't want us destroyed. We humans are special to her, Ghile. I think that is why she only allows the descendants of those who awakened her to even hear her dreams. So was our creator, Haurtu," Adon said.

Ghile flinched at the name and made a protective gesture over his heart. "Don't say that name, Adon. The devourer will hear you, if you speak his name."

Adon smiled as if at some inner joke.

"It isn't funny, Adon," Ghile said.

"I agree. It isn't funny. The people from the Great Purge go to some endless slumber instead of where they should go, all because the other gods were jealous of Haurtu. Not just them, either. Why am I there? I think it is because I was culled. There are many others there who were culled, maybe all of them."

Ghile just stared and couldn't form words to reply. He had never heard Adon speak of the gods and the histories like this. What had he seen in those dreamings? His fear gave him focus. "Adon, the Devourer ate his own brothers and sisters," Ghile said after a time.

Adon grimaced. "Don't be silly, Ghile, he didn't make a soup out of them and nibble on their bones."

Ghile pictured a giant monster gorging itself on body parts, sucking on a leg with wet, slapping lips. "That is what the histories say," Ghile tried to defend himself. He wasn't sure why, but he somehow felt his position was the right one, so he defended it.

"No, he did take in some of the other gods, but he made them a part of him. Like when you pour two mugs of water into a bigger mug. He was trying to become the All Father, to join Allwyn in the dreaming. It was what she wanted her children to do. The others were just too afraid to try."

Ghile made a face like he just tasted something sour. "He wanted to handfast with his mother?"

Adon gave him a look, as if he thought Ghile was being dense on purpose. It was the same look he used to give him when Ghile would fail at one of the chores Adon had explained to him for the fourth time. "She created the gods, Ghile. So yes, to us she is their mother, but not to them. To them she is just a powerful being who brought them into existence with a purpose. But one she never shared with them. Haurtu was known as Haurtu the Wise, he was a god of thinking and learning." Adon's face was filled with wonder as he looked back into his memories.

"Ghile, you should have seen the cities and temples we built in his name. Great libraries filled with books." Adon saw the look of confusion on Ghile's face at the mention of books. "Tablets like the dwarves use to save words. Words for others to say later.

"I saw some dreamings of those cities, Ghile. They were incredible. Some of the dreamers were great priests of Haurtu and I learned many things from them. We are not a cursed race, Ghile. We are being punished by the dwarves because we were created by Haurtu and the other gods were jealous of his ambition."

"If he was right and Allwyn wanted her children, I mean, her creations to consume one another and join her, why did she create so many of them in the first place?" Ghile thought he had made a fine point and leaned back to see how Adon would answer it.

If Adon was bothered, he didn't show it. "It all makes sense, Ghile. Look at Allwyn. The creatures that live on her. Everything struggles to survive. Everything learns to grow and become stronger or is destroyed and consumed by those who do. If this is the way of things in the great All Mother's dreaming, then one would think that was the way she would do it. The way she would find her equal?"

Ghile thought about it and could understand what Adon meant, maybe even agreed with him a little. But he just couldn't get the image out of his mind of those big, smacking lips.

19

Journey to Lakeside

HE warmer summer winds from the lowlands pushed into Upper Vale, heralding the short summer's arrival. The days were at their longest and the residents of Last Hamlet took advantage of the extra light. The snow could still be seen on the uppermost peaks and the top of the Horn, but the grasses down in the valley were lush and green.

Last Hamlet was a bustle of activity in preparation for the annual journey down to Lakeside. Ox drawn carts were loaded with the prepared fleeces ready for market and the annual tithing to the dwarves. Those who couldn't make the journey on foot rode on the carts among the fleece, the young ones waving up at them as they played amongst the carts.

The handful of boys of age to take the test of man-hood ran races and fought mock battles against each other, boasting how well they were going to do. No one mentioned the dwarf's Rite of Attrition that always occurred after the tests. It was a known risk all took. Other than Adon, there had been only three other humans culled as long as anyone could remember. Some felt it was a small price to pay, considering it was what kept the dwarves from exterminating humans completely.

The last few weeks had passed quickly for Ghile since he had awoken from his experience in the ruins. Both Almoriz and Riff had ignored his father's request to leave Last Hamlet, and even now Riff was fastening the last of his sacks on their mule.

Almoriz sat on the ground nearby, smoking his pipe and watching the young with the fascination and patience the elderly always seem to have for them. He looked at Ghile and Ghile hurriedly looked away, turning back to his father's cart and acting as if he were checking the goods were secured.

The sorcerer and his apprentice had both been acting differently since the incident at the ruins. Ghile did not understand why Riff refused to admit where he'd found him and even when he caught Riff alone one night a couple weeks back, he'd insisted he hadn't seen a statue. Ghile had tried to return to the ruins again, but between Riff, Almoriz, his father and his mother, he hadn't been left alone long enough to slip away. His father had filled any free time he would have normally enjoyed in the summer with training in both spear and shield, making him run up and down the Vale, and collecting stones and moving them to the pasture walls without the use of the cart. All this to improve his strength and prepare him for his tests.

Gar and Bralf had avoided him since the ruins. Ghile figured they feared he would tell Ecrec about their involvement in his son being found unconscious in the forbidden ruins. He finally had to admit to having fallen in the dark and hitting his head, even though anyone who had seen him while he slept knew his head was not hurt.

The alternative was to say he passed out from fright at becoming lost and that did not appeal to him at all. The teasing he had grown up with concerning his clumsiness and height were bad enough, but he had grown used to it. He even had to admit the bullying he suffered at the hands of Gar and Bralf didn't stop him from looking back at his young life with fondness.

He knew when he returned home, he would return a man and his childhood would be behind him. He would be a man. Free to marry and build his own home. Of course, those were the furthest things from his mind, even though he knew it was one of the main things his mother and the other mothers of boys about to take the test would be thinking of. Besides the markets, they would gather with women from the other settlements to look for potential handfasting matches. It was not unheard of to have a boy complete his test and then be handfasted off by parents looking for grandchildren or the new daughter's dowry.

But would he return home? What if they made him strip off his clothes? He didn't remember it being part of the test, but what if they did? Would anyone notice the raised circle in the middle of his chest? Would the culler know? Is this what they looked for? Ghile thought about the stories of Haurtu, the Hungering God, who had gone mad, killed and then eaten the other gods.

He worried what was happening to him was what the dwarves watched for. Had Adon been in the ruins and found the statue, too? Was that why he was in that dream place now? If he was culled like Adon, would he go there forever?

He thought about it. It was a good place and other than that ridiculous shadow that skulked around the island and occasionally made pathetic attempts to attack Adon or lure Ghile off into the woods, it was a type of paradise.

His time spent with Adon had only helped to remind him how much he had missed his brother. Adon was different than before. More focused and tended to talk a lot more, but that was to be expected. He had been taken and culled by the dwarves and was now on that island forever.

The things Ghile had learned still fascinated him. He could move things near him with a thought. Small things only and only one at a time. He still wasn't as good as Adon, who could lift many things at once. Ghile carried a small pouch with the stones he had gathered to practice with during the rare times he was left to himself. He smiled and touched the pouch.

Almost like a sorcerer's pouch, he thought. But unlike Riff and Almoriz, he did not require a source to work this new power Adon had taught him. Though, he did tend to get a serious headache if he practiced too long or tried to mind touch, as Adon called it, more than he was capable of.

It was odd, touching objects with his mind. It was like reaching out and touching something with his hand. He could feel the texture of it, the stones for example, were hard and smooth in his mind. It also helped to mind touch something if he had touched it with his hands before. The more familiar he was with something the easier it was to mind touch.

The best trick he had discovered was the ability to throw the stones by mind touching them. He could hurl all five of them, one after the other, in quick succession, more accurately and harder than he ever would have been able to throw them with his hand.

He thought about the manhood test and looked forward to seeing how his new abilities would help him complete it. He was much more confident now and found he hadn't tripped recently and always knew when to duck before bumping his head into something. He thought he must be getting the confidence of a man. Maybe that was what the others were noticing when he caught them staring at him when they thought he wasn't looking.

The creaking wheels of the cart brought him out of his reverie. They were moving. People laughed and chatted as they all began the journey down to Lakeside. Ghile was sorry Uncle Toren hadn't joined them. He had heard the other two fangs who had come through on their way to the festival say he shouldn't be far behind him. They had seen him not two days before. He was going to make one last run along the Horn and then head down. They would probably run into him along the way.

Ghile wondered if he could confide in Uncle Toren. Adon had been explicit when he said to tell no one, but Ghile doubted if that included Uncle Toren. He had always been there with a smile and an understanding nod. Ghile thought about this as he walked. Yes, he could trust Uncle Toren. He would tell him on the way to the festival.

20

On the Horn

UK concentrated hard to keep the worgs from eating the human. They had the man cornered against the back wall of the cavern Muk had claimed as his lair on the ugly mountain. Its entrance was large enough for the worgs to enter and there was a ledge not too far away, where he could look down onto the boy's village.

He had been planning how to get to the boy when the worgs had smelled this bothersome human following their tracks. Muk toyed with the idea of letting them go on and eat him. His attempts to control the man as he could the worgs had failed miserably. He had jumped up and down for a long time after that failure.

Even now the man watched him warily through his one good eye. He didn't look well, he had been bitten in several places as the worgs had subdued and dragged him here. But, Muk would not kill him yet. He looked like the boy. Muk had been so excited at first when they had captured him. He thought he had the boy, but it was not him. Just some guard who must be related. The dream goblin said he could be of use, so he was going to keep him alive for now.

Muk sat on the opposite side of the cave from the man. He had long since gone through his gear and claimed his metal knife and bow. Muk particularly liked the bow. He kept the metal knife, which shined pretty, but he would never want to get close enough to something to have to use it.

He rubbed the stone in his chest as he often did when he thought. He wished he spoke the man's language, but the man had not said anything to him he could understand. Dumb man thing, maybe he should let his worgs eat him.

Bloody Maw came trotting back into the cave and made straight for Muk. The other members of the pack marked his passage across the sloping cavern.

Muk jumped excitedly from one foot to the other. "Well? Well?"

"Master, he is not in the human dwellings. Very few humans there. Are you sure that is his lair?" Bloody Maw sprawled down on the floor, tongue lolling out as he panted.

"Yes, that is his lair," Muk said. Where was the thrice-damned boy? He wanted his stone! The dream goblin had shown him the boy once he had arrived on the mountain. He could see his face even now.

Muk shook and began jumping again. That human boy had his stone. He was supposed to be in that village. Muk stopped jumping and contented himself with stabbing the dagger against the rock floor as he grumbled. He would just have to have patience, like the dream goblin told him. The boy would return. But now Muk had to figure out how to get to the boy without having to fight the entire village.

Maybe they could go down there now and kill those that were there. Bloody Maw had said there were only a few. But would that warn the boy? Muk had to do this right. He would wait for the boy to return and then lure him out of his village somehow.

Muk sat there on the cavern floor, stabbing his new dagger into the stone. He thought of the powers he would have once he had killed the boy and taken his stone. He wondered if he would have to eat all of him, or just touch him as he had the man statue in the ruins? He doubted the boy would hold still while the stone crawled out of him. Muk displayed all his small pointy teeth with the grin that came to him as he thought of the boy flailing under the pain.

He considered Bloody Maw and the other worgs. He could send them in to grab the boy. The others could attack the rest of the village while Bloody Maw grabbed the boy and brought him to Muk. Muk gnashed his teeth. For that plan to work, Muk would have to go down there with the pack. He examined his new bow. He didn't like the idea of being on the receiving end of a human arrow. He might also lose a good number of his worgs to those humans and their dogs.

Muk stopped stabbing the ground and smiled.

Their dogs. Now there was an idea.

21

In Everyone's Best Interest

AIDEL could feel the blood rising to her cheeks. After the trouble back in Redwood, she knew this return home to the Cradle was going to be difficult. She had been raised, like every other child in the Cradle, to fear the Nordlah Barbarians.

She had been taught the land below the Drops was a dangerous wilderness where the tribes of barbarians and orcs constantly fought. If the barbarians and orcs didn't kill you, there were forest trolls along the plain's border and all types of giant cats that would be happy to oblige.

She could understand her kinsmen's dislike of her shieldwarden, but she had thought that title would be enough to make them look past Two Elks' heritage. The ceremony around the binding of a druid and her shieldwarden was a sacred one. She was beginning to understand that most just assumed the daughters chose their shieldwarden. But why would she bring this kind of trouble on herself?

"Do not presume to know my business, Magister," Gaidel said. She could feel Two Elks behind the thick chair and was thankful for his presence.

Magister Obudar cleared his throat and leaned back. Dwarves always thought before they spoke. This one had made an art of it. "I do not presume to know your business, but I do presume to question it when it effects the Cradle. Your shieldwarden was ill chosen, Daughter Gaidel."

Gaidel pretended to smooth her green robes. She could not argue that point, she had thought it many times since the binding herself. But, she was not going to admit it to Magister Obudar. "I am not comfortable with this conversation, Magister Obudar." She was uncomfortable with this whole situation.

She had been approached as soon as she and Two Elks entered Lakeside, and shuffled into the Bastion through its dock entrance and straight into this small windowless room somewhere on the ground floor. There was entirely too much stone and not enough light here for her comfort.

"If you asked me to attend an audience to talk about my shieldwarden, we are finished." Gaidel made to stand.

The two dwarven guards who stood by the door tensed, chain sliding against plate armor, as did the two guards behind Obudar's chair.

117

The magister raised one of his thick jeweled hands. "Be at peace, Daughter Gaidel."

Gaidel sensed, rather than saw Two Elks' irritation. She could feel his eagerness to test himself against the four dwarven guards. She breathed deeply and thought calming thoughts. It would only make it worse if Two Elks fed on her unease.

"I would have waited to speak with Mother Brambles, but time was of the essence and I asked to speak with the first druid who could be found," the magister said. "I only wish you to remind your sisters and more specifically Mother Brambles, to help keep the peace during the festival and particularly during the Rite of Attrition."

Gaidel frowned. Something was wrong. The druids knew the dwarves of the Cradle held their rite during the summer festival for just that purpose. She also knew the rites rarely resulted in an actual culling. What was the magister not telling her? The dwarves rarely did anything in haste, so this rushed secret meeting meant something was sorely amiss.

"We are well aware of our responsibilities in keeping the balance in the Cradle, Magister Obudar. Is there something more you could share with us to help towards that goal?" Gaidel said.

The silence drifted on in the impromptu meeting room as the magister stared at her. She could almost see his mind at work. She would indeed find Mother Brambles as soon as she could.

The magister finally leaned forward over steepled fingers. "The knight justice sent by the Temple of

Daomur has spent most of his time performing his holy duties upon the Nordlah Plains."

Gaidel gasped. "Why would they send him?" She had seen first-hand the violent conflicts between Two Elks' people and the cullers. She forgot protocol as fear for her people crowded her thoughts. "It makes no sense; the Cradle follows all your laws, even the ridiculous—"

"You presume much, Druid!" Magister Obudar said rising from his chair.

Gaidel heard Two Elks' shield slide off his shoulder and she rose quickly from her chair. Sudden movement echoed through the small room as weapons were readied and feet shifted into defensive stances. The two guards near the magister were now at his side.

Obudar regained his composure and raised his hands. "Everyone be calm. Guards, stand down."

Gaidel waited as the guards returned to their stations and the magister to his seat.

"The deal is made. The Temple has chosen and we all must make do," the magister eventually said.

Gaidel ignored him and turned to Two Elks. "We are leaving." She walked past him and towards the door. The other two guards stepped in front of it and stared past her to the magister.

"We need to find Mother Brambles with all haste," Gaidel announced to the room.

"Escort Daughter Gaidel and her shieldwarden out through the dock entrance," the magister said.

The two door guards slammed mailed fists against their chests in response.

"Escort them to the main gate, as well," the magister added. "I would not want anything to happen to them in Lakeside."

Gaidel made to rebuke the order then thought better of it. She resented being thrown out of town, but, grudgingly admitted to herself it was the prudence of the action she resented most. She had to find Mother Brambles and seek her counsel.

22

The Festival

HILE was worried. Uncle Toren had not met up with the caravan. Ghile had stared at the pockmarked face of the Horn, searching its surface for any sign of his uncle as the caravan made its way down the valley.

Each time others joined the caravan, Ghile thought he saw Uncle Toren among them. He could see Toren's big smile as he waved to Ghile, fresh stories of his latest adventures ready to share. But each time it turned out to be someone else.

He knew he was not the only one worried, he often caught his father and mother looking towards the mountain as well. He even heard some of the men commenting on it at the first night's fire. Ghile thought back to all the stories his uncle had told him, about the dangers in the mountains surrounding the Cradle. Ghile hoped he was all right. His uncle wouldn't miss his manhood tests without good reason.

Ghile entertained the idea of going to look for him again. He fingered his pouch of stones. *Am I mad*? All he would do is get himself killed up there. *But things were different now,* he told himself. He was different. He had his powers to protect him.

Ghile needed to take the test and pass the culling. He noticed his mother atop the cart. She gripped her scarf tightly, something she did when she was worried. Of course she was worried. She had made a journey just like this four years ago and lost her first born. Ghile hoped she wasn't going to lose another.

They reached Lakeside in the morning of the third day. He had seen the deep blue waters of Crystal Lake well before they reached the town situated along its rocky shore. The rows of steep-arched long houses and muddy streets were a sharp contrast to the other settlements of the Cradle. In the middle of it all, the Bastion rose like a stone guardian, visible well beyond the town walls.

Ghile saw a large flying creature circling lazily around the Bastion's upper crenellations. *The culler's mount,* he thought. Everyone talked about the flying beasts the cullers' rode upon. Gifts from the gods, it was said, just like their powers. The same powers they used to decide if you were to be removed from the race of man, Ghile supposed. He shuddered as the reality of what was to come settled on his very young shoulders. *I am not a chosen of Haurtu,* he repeated to himself. *That is not where my powers come from. I found an ancient stone that allows me to meet my brother in my dreams. He can talk to the ancestors and they have shared their secrets with him and he has shared them with me. This is different.*

Ghile tried to convince himself everything would be all right as their caravan pulled their carts off the north road, just outside the main wooden gates.

Tents of all sizes and shapes dotted the fields along the outside of the huge wooden palisade that walled Lakeside. Musicians wandered, performing amongst the tents. Children ran in small groups, screaming and laughing, feeding off the excitement. Ghile heard the music from at least four different performers. A piper and drummer played a hopping jig near a large, multicolored tent, while another group played violins accompanied by pipes, a song Ghile was unfamiliar with.

A couple of girls his age walked past him, deep in whispered conversation, interspersed with fits of giggles. They both had their hair wreathed in flowers. Ghile knew this meant they were of handfasting age. One, with hair the color of an evening fire, looked at him and smiled. The flame haired girl broke into another giggle and whispered hurriedly to her friend who then turned to stare. He looked about for something to do and heard their eruption of laughter. He was sure his face was now as red as her hair.

Ghile helped his father and mother set up their tent and move the goods they weren't tithing into it. While Tia played with her straw baby, Elana began organizing things and making the tent where they would be for the next few days, a home.

With a quarter of their fleeces on the cart, Ghile and his father headed into town. The smells of fresh baked bread and sizzling meat competed with roasting nuts and the sour tang of spilled ale to draw Ghile's attention. Food stalls crowded together along the tall palisade, their vendors adding their voices to the barrage of smells to draw the attention of the revelers.

"Scared, Son?" Ecrec asked as they made their way through the crowd.

"Sorry, Father?" Ghile had been taking so many things in, he wasn't sure which one his father was referring to.

"The Rites of Attrition. The culler. Your Manhood test."

Ghile looked up at the culler's flying mount, still circling their destination and considered. Of course he was scared. He could feel the fear waiting just below the surface, but looking into his father's eyes, he knew he couldn't tell him that. Ecrec needed his son to be strong, like him. If Ghile told him what he really felt, he didn't think his father would understand.

"No, Father. I will make you proud."

Ecrec smiled and nodded. He gave Ghile a firm pat on the shoulder and shook him a little. "You will do fine, Ghile. Then we will go home."

They entered the central square and turned onto the main thoroughfare of Market Street. Market Street lead straight to the Bastion and then on to the docks. They reached the line of tithers stretched down Market Street well before they reached the Bastion. Ecrec guided their cart to the end of it and greeted the men in front of them. Ghile took in the sights and sounds around him as they started the slow stop and go pace of the line.

"What do the dwarves do with what we give them?" Ghile asked when they were near enough to the front to see men unloading their goods onto the stone landing at the base of the Bastion.

"I have been told they take what they need and store it in the Bastion, the rest they send to their capital city," Ecrec said.

Ghile strained to catch a glimpse of the dwarves. He finally saw a couple of them seated at a stone bench on the edge of the platform. As the men unloaded goods, those working on the platform would take them, sort them, and then report to the dwarves, who then scratched on something on the table. Ghile had asked about this before. They were writing. A way of taking words and keeping them. If you understood the way to write the words, then you could speak them off what they were written on.

His people didn't have a need for writing. If you had something to say, then you just said it. Why would they need to write down words for what they collected? They had it there before them. Ghile shook his head. He did not understand dwarves.

Ghile continued to study the two dwarves. One was incredibly old, the hair on his head completely gone, while his beard reminded Ghile of a river flowing over gray stones. It ran down to disappear behind the table, Ghile could just see the end wisps dangling near the old dwarf's thick boots.

The other was much younger. He couldn't tell how old a dwarf really was, but this one had reddish brown hair that only just came off his chin and a nose that took up too much of his face.

They both seem to be as wide as they were tall. Ghile always marveled at how broad dwarfs were. They reminded him of tree trunks. The one feature they all shared was their expressions. They all looked bored. Like they didn't enjoy anything. At least, not like humans did. These two looked content to be doing what they did, but they didn't seem excited about it.

When it was their turn, Ghile helped his father hand the tied bundles of fleece up to the men on the platform. The younger dwarf glanced up from his tablets and scratchings, and Ghile thought the dwarf took his measure in that one stoic glance.

What do you see when you look at me?

The young dwarf was not forthcoming with any answers and turned back to his work.

"Name and residence?" the young dwarf said. His voice reminded Ghile of one of those large frame drums the troubadours played.

"Ecrec of Last Hamlet," Ecrec said. With a nod of the elderly dwarf's head they were done. Their keepers were sated for another year.

But the tithing was not the only effect the dwarves were having on his people, Ghile learned as they went on to trade with their first city merchant.

"What is this?" Ecrec asked.

The merchant, his expansive waist filling his side of the table, stopped and looked up to see Ecrec gesturing at the coins he was counting out. "You can trust that this is top price, Ecrec of Last Hamlet," the Merchant said, misunderstanding.

"No, the coin. Where is your wife? I want red and white cloth for this bundle, not these dwarven coins."

The merchant sighed and ran a handkerchief over his damp pink scalp. "I don't understand why I have to keep explaining this to you and your kin, Ecrec. I'll buy all of your fleece from you. The whole lot. Then, you take these coins I have given you and you use them to buy your goods from the other merchants. My wife is selling her cloth just one street over."

Ecrec stared at the coins and then stared at the merchant. Ghile didn't think the man could sweat anymore, but he was wrong. He positively leaked.

"Listen, Ecrec, please just use the coins. It is the law. We have to trade in their coin. It is how they keep track of things."

Ecrec set his jaw and was shaking his head. Ghile swallowed and wished now more than ever his uncle had been with them. Toren was always good at keeping his father calm.

"It is the law," the merchant repeated.

"Father?" Ghile said, trying to think of what else he could say.

Ecrec scooped up the coins and thrust them into Ghile's hands. "Here, boy," he said and then turned to the merchant. "How do I know how much I have?"

The merchant exhaled and smiled nervously. "Here, Ecrec of Last Hamlet, I'll explain them to you."

The merchant sorted the coins out into their different sizes and shapes. They all had a small circular hole in them. The largest ones were rectangular and heavier than the rest. Ghile could see five of those. He listened as the merchant explained how they were worth less as they got smaller.

It took Ecrec time, but he eventually got the hang of using the dwarven coin and at the end of the first day, they returned to their tent on the outskirts of Lakeside with a good amount of supplies.

Ghile was exhausted and needed to get a good night's sleep before his manhood test tomorrow. He quickly drifted off and dreamed of giggling, red-haired girls.

23

The Welcome

ELCOME citizens and humans of the Cradle to the summer festival!" Magister Obudar said over the gathered crowds. Cheers erupted around him. He stood on the wooden platform that was erected in the center of the festival field each summer for this event. He looked down at his clansmen gathered closest around him.

They were citizens of the empire and thus were always given priority over the humans. Like him, they were dressed in their finest earth tone robes. The early morning sun caused their many pieces of jewelry to cast off multifaceted beams of light.

Beyond them the sea of human faces stretched into the distance. He could see the occasional tonsure cuts of the druids, their blue tattoos differencing them from the others. They would help keep the others in line.

"We gather together again in peace and prosperity," he continued. It seemed all the Cradle had come together for the event. It was always good to remind them how lucky they all were.

"The Cradle of the Gods is blessed by Daomur. By choosing to live under his laws and the stewardship of his chosen people, you have ensured this. For this I, and the other citizens of the Cradle, thank you." Obudar said.

The respectful clapping around the platform was again drowned out by the enthusiastic cheers of the humans. He sighed at their exuberance. Such an emotional people. The citizens would take in the market stalls and then return to the Bastion. They had no interests in the manhood tests or what went on in the field at night. More like animals, at times, these humans. Not their fault, though. They were descended from the exiled god. Obudar gave silent thanks to Daomur for being born a dwarf.

"Enjoy your festival and celebrate. His word is Law."

"His word is law," was echoed back at him. He noticed more than one disapproving look from the citizens at the exuberance with which some of the humans shouted it. More like a cheer for the festivities to begin than the reminder it was.

With his official duties done, he made his way down off the platform. His guards, their plated armor reflecting the sun, waited at the base of the stairs to escort him back to the Bastion. He soon lost sight of the city walls. His guards parted the sea of humans, but could do nothing about the oppressive heat and smell that remained in their wake. Luckily, he was heading back to the Bastion and the humans made their way in the opposite direction, to the forest's edge where the manhood tests would soon begin.

The noise was deafening. Many were already drinking. They would celebrate well into the night. He thought about the profits he would make from the tax on beer. The festival was always profitable, but Obudar was glad he would not be needed again until tomorrow afternoon to oversee the Rites of Attrition. The thought of some of the things these humans got up to at their celebrations was enough to make a graybeard blush.

He was also glad the knight justice was nowhere to be seen. Finngyr's dislike of humans was beneficial in that it kept him in the Bastion for the majority of his stay. He would have to visit with the knight justice one more time to remind him of how the Elders wanted the Rite to be handled, for all the good it would do.

24

The Manhood Tests

HE initiates gathered in the circular clearing created by a line of wooden poles. Each pole, twice the size of a man, held back a river of cheering faces like a dam ready to give. Ghile and the other youths stretched and bounced with infectious eagerness.

Mother Brambles emerged from the forest and slowly made her way down the pole-lined passage leading to the initiates, her gigantic bear lumbering behind her. Ghile and the others' stretching and posturing was forgotten as they all stopped to watch the two approach. Those in the crowd closest to the poles fell silent as the matriarch of all druids passed. The bear roared, silencing the rest. Only the cries of a few babies, brought on by the roar, remained.

"Hear my words," Mother Brambles called out. "As is our tradition, these boys take this test of manhood to prove their worth to their people and show respect for the old ways. Those who evade capture do so through the All Mother's protection. Those she deems not yet ready to be men will be denied her protection and left to their fates."

Behind Ghile, men of the Cradle jeered and whooped. Ghile had seen boys carried out of the forest bruised and bloodied from their struggles to escape the hunters. He did not know which was worse, the beating, or the humiliation of getting caught.

Ghile looked from the hunters to the other initiates taking the test. His eyes locked with Gar's. A smile, which never reached Gar's eyes, slowly stretched across his face. Before Ghile would have been terrified. But, not anymore. Ghile returned a smile of his own and motioned for Gar to bring his best. A moment of confusion passed over Gar's face before it was replaced by one of anger.

So, I'll have to avoid the hunters and watch out for Gar and Bralf at the same time. So be it. At that moment, Ghile felt more alive and ready to take on the world than ever before. *How could you want me to miss this, Adon?*

"Prepare yourselves," Mother Brambles said, looking over the initiates as if testing them then and there.

Hear me, All Mother. I am not one of your daughters and don't know if you even really care about this test, but I ask for your protection. I am ready to be a man. Ghile swallowed, trying to clear his mind. He knew had to keep his head about him if he was going to pass this ordeal. Ghile lowered his long frame and set his feet, feeling the ground firmly beneath them.

As one, Mother Bramble's club came down and the river breached its dam. The initiates bolted for the forest to the sound of the cheering crowd and the hunter's clubs banging against shields, all working to drive the initiates on.

Ghile ran.

He ran past a blur of faces and waving hands. The forest loomed before him, ready to swallow him and his youth in one shadowed gulp.

All the things his father and Uncle Toren taught him fought for precedence. Most importantly, he tried to remember how long he had before Mother Brambles released the hunters to give chase.

As soon as they passed the edge of the forest, the other two dozen initiates veered off and headed in as many directions. Ghile went straight. He was going to wait until he was well out of sight of the hunters before adjusting his course.

He had some decisions to make. He had laid awake many nights, but could never decide which the best course of action was. He was out of time. He had to make a decision.

He had gone far enough in and stopped, watching the others continue past him. He felt a hard shove and stumbled into the rough trunk of a tree. Catching himself, he saw Gar continue deeper into the forest.

"Giving up already?" Bralf called as he ran past Ghile, trying to keep up with Gar.

Ghile swallowed down his anger and watched to make sure they kept running. When Bralf and Gar were no more than movement in the distance he pushed them from his thoughts and breathed deep. He took in his surroundings.

The forest was full of deep summer greenery. Uncle Toren had said that would be to his favor, but fast movements would still draw attention. Ghile looked around for something that would help hide his tracks. Not too far from where he stood, a tree had given under the weight of years and finally cracked, falling to the forest floor. Already moss and the All Mother's children had begun to reclaim it.

That would do.

Ghile walked to the fallen tree and climbed its surface. The moss was dry, not slippery as he thought it might be. Making his way along the trunk for a good distance, he stopped when he spotted a clump of boulders a short distance away. He moved a little higher up the trunk and then, judging he had enough height, scanned the forest once more.

He was alone.

He focused his mind and concentrated on producing force from his hands as he had done so many times before in his dreams. He was aware of every sound around him. He felt the wind whisper against the hair on his bare arms. He had to focus.

Raising his arms to their limits above him, he finally felt force stretch out above him. He exerted more will and could sense the shield's edges stretching out, forming a large, slightly curved plate. When

135

he couldn't stretch it any further he leaped towards the boulders.

He felt the shield catch air as he fell forward more than down, drifting quickly.

He could see he was going to make it, but he was coming in much faster and higher than he had anticipated. The wide grey stones shot past beneath him. Ghile wished he could concentrate on more than one shield at a time. He had to decide quickly, or he would sail past his target.

He released the shield from his mind and the one above him vanished at the same instant. The sudden feeling of falling caught his breath. He focused on the thicker force shield and pushed it out from his legs.

Just in time, he felt it stretch out from him as the resistance of the boulder's angled surface pushed against it. He was getting better at keeping his balance while doing this and he release the shield. His feet landed soundlessly against the stone.

Ghile scrambled across one boulder to the next. He had an idea. Once he reached the last one, he again concentrated on the force shield and pushed it down and out of his feet. He stepped off the boulder and took a few lumbering steps forward, swinging his arms for balance.

His mind ached with pressure. He felt like something had reached into his head and was crushing his brain. He barely had the strength of will to maintain the two small force shields under his feet. He didn't understand why two should be harder than one. Combined, they were far smaller in size than the flat shield he used to float down like a leaf or the thick one he used to slow his falls. The image of the two separate force shields pulled and slipped in his mind like a freshly caught fish. When it became too much, he released it and fell the last few inches to the forest floor.

He turned back to look at his handiwork. If anyone had seen him, he would have looked as if he had flown from the fallen tree to those boulders, like those squirrels his uncle sometimes killed on his patrols. They had a thin membrane between their legs and it was this that had given Ghile the idea in the first place.

He wondered if he could extend the force from his sides like them, instead of out of his hands and feet. He did not see why not, though now was not the time to try. Creating two shields at once had mentally exhausted him. He had covered a good deal of ground and felt that would do to lose anyone who tried tracking him from the festival field.

He headed deeper into the wood. He couldn't help but laugh as he ran. The confidence he felt wanted to boil out of him. Ghile had feared this test for so long and now, with his new found abilities, he felt for the first time he was going to survive. As he ran deeper into the forest, he thought of how proud his father was going to be.

25

Discoveries

IFF watched Ghile and the other initiates dash into the Redwood like fleeing rabbits. Those men who were not blood relations of the initiates, and still young enough to think chasing them through the forest seemed good sport, yelled and banged their shields to drive the initiates on. They kept one eye on the forest and another on Mother Brambles, waiting for her to unleash them.

All muscle and no brain.

They knew as well as he did she would allow the initiates a good head start. But they slathered and whined, wanting to give chase, all the same. The similarities between him and the hunters chafed his pride.

Riff turned and made his way through the throng. He needed to find Master Almoriz. He, too, had done as he was told and kept an eye on Ghile. Riff liked Ghile well enough. He felt beholden to look out for him after Adon had been culled, even without Master Almoriz's direction. He and Adon had always gotten along well on his visits and Adon had been the closest thing Riff had to a true friend.

He didn't think Master Almoriz had meant for him to follow Ghile into the wood. He wasn't about to strip down to his waist and be painted up like the rest of those louts. He had already taken the test and that was one time too many. He was not volunteering to spend a night crawling through the woods chasing boys out of hiding holes and trees. That was not his idea of an evening well spent.

He still wished the old sorcerer would explain to him what was going on. He had told Master Almoriz how he had found Ghile on the floor of that hidden shrine. The inhabitants of the Cradle feared the ancient ruins and if that wasn't enough to keep them away, dwarven law prohibited humans from trespassing in them.

There were not enough dwarves in the Cradle to do more than guard the Bastion and count the tithes the cradlers poured into it. Riff had no respect for the little walking blocks of stone. Dwarves were a necessary evil as far as he was concerned.

Master Almoriz always sent him into the ruins when they were staying in Last Hamlet. He always found good stones and the occasional cache of metal bits there, but little else. He usually just found a nice place to catch a nap.

He had long since come to the conclusion that there was nothing of interest in those ruins. He thought he had scoured them thoroughly enough on previous visits. He could not believe Adon's lanky little brother had found a hidden shrine to some forgotten stonechosen.

He had heard the screaming somewhere deeper in the ruins. He recalled feeling a twinge of jealousy when he came upon the trap door hanging open in the middle of the room.

The room was a crossroads of sorts and he had passed through it many times. How could he have missed the trap door? He made a mental note to pry off the metal handle after he gotten to the bottom of those screams.

Now that he was at the room, the screams had stopped. The light from the everflame he held danced off the walls and the open trap door. He had little doubt where the screams had come from. He had recognized Ghile's voice in those screams and called his name from the top of the stairway.

There was no answer. He held the everflame before him and made his way down. He kept the words to the flame strike spell on his lips. Master Almoriz had told him he was not allowed to use the spell unless it was a life or death situation. This qualified. He was definitely going to set fire to anything that appeared and sort out the particulars later.

He saw Ghile's crumpled body sprawled out on the floor in front of a statue of a stonechosen. Riff put his back against a wall as soon as he reached the foot of the stairs and used the everflame to illuminate the room.

He recognized it as a shrine and didn't see any other occupants except Ghile. He knelt down and felt Ghile's face. He was breathing, but he burned with a fever. He checked Ghile for any obvious injuries. What had happened to him? There was nothing obvious and Ghile's breathing seemed normal enough. He gave Ghile a shake and called his name. Ghile wouldn't wake up.

Riff examined the stonechosen. He recognized the swirling stone pattern from Master Almoriz's lessons. He had seen similar relics in other ruins, but never this large and well preserved.

He felt along the statue and its base for any loose stones that might reveal a hidden compartment. The stone too was hot to the touch. He glanced down at Ghile. Had he set off some ancient trap? He knew the dwarves sometimes trapped ruins, to punish those who disobeyed their laws. No dwarf worth their beard would have left this statue intact, though. If it was a trap, it was not dwarf made.

He had to get Ghile out of here and seal this room. He made a thorough search for anything of value. Then, having carried Ghile back out of the ruins he returned and removed the valuable metal handle. That done, he found some heavy stones to cover the trap door. That would have to do. Now to get Ghile back up to Last Hamlet.

He stumbled into Last Hamlet at dusk with Ghile across his shoulder. He didn't know why, but he felt guilty when Elana burst into tears at the sight of her unconscious child. Ecrec took his son and barraged Riff with questions. He would have liked to have had time to speak alone with Master Almoriz, who was standing there in the crowd that soon formed. He didn't have time. "I was down in the lower fields and heard screams coming from the old ruins," Riff said.

"What was he doing in those ruins?" Ecrec grumbled, carrying Ghile towards his home.

"If the dwarves would have found him! Oh, Ecrec, I can't lose another." Elana followed closely through the crowd, carrying a wide-eyed Tia who still didn't seem to know how to act.

"Not sure, but I found him just inside like this. He wouldn't wake up," Riff said.

Riff followed until they reached their roundhouse. Master Almoriz followed the family inside. "Wait here, apprentice," Almoriz said, closing both halves of the door behind him.

Riff lingered outside the roundhouse with the crowd, explaining again and again as other members of Last Hamlet were drawn by the crowd.

Master Almoriz had emerged later and informed everyone Ghile was going to be all right and needed his rest. He then took Riff aside. "Tell me what happened, Apprentice. Do not omit any detail, no matter how insignificant you think it to be," his master said.

Riff retold the events of what happened and Master Almoriz listened intently. When he finished, the old sorcerer remained lost in thought for some time before responding.

"Your story is to remain the same as you told it to his parents. When Ghile awakes—"

Riff attempted to ask how he knew Ghile would awake, but Master Almoriz furrowed his thick white brows and spoke over him.

"When Ghile awakes, you will tell him the same story. Under no circumstances are you to tell him where you found him or listen to any explanation he tries to give you," Master Almoriz continued. "You will then keep an eye on him and tell me if you observe anything odd."

"Master Almoriz, I don't understand. What happened to him?" Riff asked.

"Boy, it is not something for you to understand. Now is not the time for your incessant questions. You will do as I tell you, Apprentice." Master Almoriz stared until he seemed confident Riff understood.

"Tomorrow you will take me to this shrine." Then Almoriz disappeared into Ecrec's home.

Riff lowered his head and turned his palms upward. "Yes, Master Almoriz."

See, I can be taught. Riff tried to unclench his jaw and breathe. Why was Master Almoriz not telling him what was going on? He was his apprentice and a damn good sorcerer.

Why was he being lied to? If Ghile had found an abandoned room when he was somewhere he shouldn't have been, and was cursed as a result, then why not just tell everyone and use it as a justifiable reason for the others to avoid the place? What was he not being told? What had Ghile stumbled upon?

143

More importantly, if the ruins were actually danger-ous, why had Master Almoriz allowed him to go there so many times on his own? Now that Riff consid-ered it, Almoriz had even encouraged his exploration. Was he supposed to find the shrine? Had his teacher wanted him to fall victim to this trap? To what end?

Riff, as usual, had more questions than answers. For now, he would do as he was told.

And so he had. Over the following months as the Cradle entered the full of summer, he had kept to his story and more importantly kept Ghile and his ques-tions at bay.

To what end, he was not sure. With each report to Master Almoriz he had gotten a thoughtful nod and, 'keep up the good work'; even when he had reported that Ghile was beginning to act suspicious and trying to find time to be alone.

Riff continued through the crowd until he finally spotted Master Almoriz near Mother Brambles. He was easy enough to see as the old druid and her hill of a cave bear still stood in the initiate's circle. Riff knew the stories regarding the giant protector of the oldest of druids and knew he was tame and under Mother Brambles' control. Well enough, but he still approached where Mother Brambles and Master Al-moriz were between him and the beast. No use taking chances. It was then that he noticed two others.

A young attractive druid, her tonsure and tattoos looked fresh, her luscious flame-colored hair long and braided. She was a beauty, to be sure. She had the soft complexion of the women of the Cradle, but her shieldwarden, who was sizing him up even now, was a Nordlah Barbarian. By Daomur's beard he was almost as big as Mother Brambles' bear! Riff wondered how the barbarian had made it this far into the cradle with his head still attached to his shoulders. He guessed the druids commanded more respect than he gave them credit for. Oh well, not his problem if the lovely young druid had poor taste in shieldwardens. He wondered what her taste in men was like.

Riff moved up to stand beside, yet slightly behind, Master Almoriz. "Master." He inclined his head and spoke the greeting softly, as to not interrupt, yet still announce his presence.

Master Almoriz and Mother Brambles were too deep in conversation to more than glance his way. The bear, barbarian, and flame-haired druid stared at him. He ignored the others but took the time to flash a rakish smile at the druid until she looked away, annoyed.

Too bad, he thought.

"Are you sure of this?" Mother Brambles was asking. Her words and demeanor had a no nonsense feel about them. This was a woman who was used to having things her way.

"If I were completely sure, he would not be here now. But, I am almost certain. I have not found enough information to know what the effects might be," Almoriz said.

Mother Brambles turned in Riff's direction and looked him over. "Things did not go according to your plans, Almoriz. But, if you are right, at least you were right about its whereabouts. I'll trust your judgment in this."

"Mother, with what I told you about the magister being worried about the culler and now this additional information, shouldn't we go and find the boy?" the young druid said.

Magister? Culler? Riff didn't know who this girl was, but she barely looked old enough to be handfasted and she definitely knew more of what was going on than he did. She didn't seem as pretty as he had first thought. She was far too tall for his liking.

Riff wanted nothing more than to ask what was going on, but he was not going to show how little he knew in front of this girl.

"No, we must know for sure and there is but one way I know to do that. You must be ready to protect him, Almoriz," Mother Brambles said, reaching back to pet the knee of her bear. "I can be nowhere near when it happens. I have sung on this and it is the way of it."

Master Almoriz stroked his beard as he looked about. "And what of the Sorcerer's Code? The display of magic it will take will reveal much."

"Events must flow their course. Your secrets will mean little if we are correct," Mother Brambles said. She poked him in the chest with her gnarled staff to drive her point home. "Balance above all things." She enunciated each word with a poke.

Master Almoriz finally nodded. "It will be as you say, Mother Brambles." He displayed his palms and bowed his head. He motioned for Riff to follow.

Mother Brambles raised a brow at Riff. Riff hadn't realized his mouth was agape.

She shook her stick at him. "Run along, young Master Riff. You will have answers to your questions soon enough."

Riff hastily closed his mouth and paid respects to Mother Brambles.

"Come, Riff. We have planning to do," Master Almoriz called over his shoulder.

Riff began to give chase then caught himself. He adjusted his robes and casually followed his master into the crowd as if it was his idea.

26

Unlikely Allies

"DO not trust that one, Mother," Gaidel said as she watched the sorcerer's apprentice saunter off into the crowd.

"If you choose not to trust every man who gives you an appraising look, Daughter Gaidel, you are going to end up distrusting half the Cradle," Mother Brambles said.

Two Elks chuckled behind her and earned a nudge in the ribs. If the barbarian noticed, he didn't show it. How could Mother Brambles think that was the reason for her distrust of him? She had barely noticed the looks the apprentice was giving her. Like most men, he thought her eyes were in her chest.

"As a druid, I do not let—" Gaidel began.

"Don't set your feathers a 'ruffle," Mother Brambles said. "It is good you do not trust Almoriz's apprentice. But, he is a part of this, make no mistake."

Mother Brambles turned and set her weight against the walking stick she was so well known for and began moving towards the wood. "Walk with me," she said.

Gaidel fell in beside her. As always, Two Elks hovered over her too close. She was not an unprotected child. "Must you follow so close? If I feel the need to sing the song, I'm sure you will sense it and you can stand on top of me then."

As usual, Two Elks just stared at her for a few moments. She still hadn't decided if he did this to translate her words or for effect, though she was beginning to strongly suspect the latter. She didn't have time for a staring contest and with clenched fists turned back to follow Mother Brambles.

"You shouldn't be so hard on your new shieldwarden, Daughter Gaidel," Mother Brambles said. "The binding is difficult on them and for a while, the emotion to guard and protect can be a strong one. Some have even confused it for other emotions," Mother Bramble explained, casting her a sidelong glance. The elderly woman's lips held a mischievous grin that would have made a Drop's Trapper blush.

Gaidel felt her face reddening and turned on Two Elks. "Don't even think it. Do you understand me?"

Two Elks continued to stare, his face impassive. "Too skinny," he finally said.

Mother Brambles found the reply quite entertaining and chuckled as she walked. Gaidel felt it best to not reply since she was obviously outnumbered. She would set the over-sized barbarian straight later.

They had no trouble moving through the crowd. Mother Brambles' bear companion could be seen easily over the heads of the revelers and all made sure to not tarry long in its path. They arrived at the edge of the wood and as if sensing this as their destination, the bear sniffed the ground and then half turned, falling over with a large exhale of air and a hefty thump.

Mother Brambles took a familiar seat on his front leg and leaned back into the shaggy brown coat. She positioned her walking stick across her lap and took in her surroundings. She looked as if she sat upon a throne and was about to hold council. "I think I will choose the boy as a fang," Mother Brambles eventually said.

"He has not even passed his manhood test, Mother."

"He will pass; I have sung as much. The question is, will he survive his culling?"

"He is to be culled?" Gaidel was shocked. What else had Mother Brambles sung about him? How deep into the song was Mother Brambles able to go?

"Yes, Daughter Gaidel. It is the only way for us to know for sure if he has been chosen."

Gaidel was still a novice druid and her skills reflected that. She had learned to enter the song and follow its course. She could hear all of nature singing along with her and could even have Allwyn's children follow her song for a short time. She felt a part of everything around her when in the song. But singing your own song against the constant pull of the All

Song was difficult and often druids would lose themselves in it and in doing so, lose that which made them who they were. What remained behind of a druid who had lost herself in the song was only a shell of what she once was, capable of only the simplest of tasks.

Mother Brambles had been the Mother Druid for longer than anyone could remember. How old she actually was, had often been a topic of debate when the druids gathered for council. But not a question anyone was foolish enough to ask her directly.

"Mother, if he has been chosen?" Gaidel ventured to ask.

"Then he is to be protected. Balance above all else, Daughter Gaidel," Mother Brambles said, as if it was the answer to everything.

"Balance above all else," she repeated, not truly understanding how all this would end in balance. "So, what are we to do about keeping the peace as Magister Obudar reminded me was our duty?" Gaidel said.

Mother Brambles watched the festivities, her wrinkled hand tapping along with the rhythm of a jovial song being performed by a group of wandering minstrels, who weaved their way through the crowd.

"What Master Obudar, and apparently you, do not understand is that the balance and peace do not always go hand in hand," Mother Brambles said.

Gaidel noticed others of her order had started to appear from the crowd and the wood behind them. They were all making their way towards them.

"We will let events unfold as they will. After the manhood tests and the choosing, I am leaving. I am going to ask all the others of the order to do so as well. Except for you, Daughter Gaidel. After Ghile of Last Hamlet survives his culling, I want you to bring him and his guardian to me."

"Survives his— his guardian?" Gaidel said.

"Yes. Your newest admirer, Child, young Master Riff." Mother Brambles chuckled and moved her head in time with the music. She waved for some of the new arrivals to come forward, bringing an end to their conversation.

As Gaidel watched Mother Brambles greet the new arrivals, she wondered how Ghile was supposed to survive his culling.

27

Everything Changes

HE sun's rays warmed his face, waking him. Ghile yawned and stretched as best he could. He wiped the sleep from his eyes. Carefully, Ghile scooted out from under the jagged rock lip he had used as a shelter and ventured a glance down the cliff's face to the forest floor far below.

The upper reaches of the Redwood stretched out before him, a mixture of angled limbs and scattered foliage. The blue of the sky Ghile could see through the leaves was washed with morning's orange and yellow hues. The wind still carried the coolness of night. Birdsong was already heavy in the air.

Numerous branches from the trees bordering the cliff swung lazily nearby. He had climbed down the short distance of the cliff as evening fell. Ghile tried to work the stiffness out of his shoulders. His stomach rumbled. It was time to find something to eat. He swung his legs over the edge and was just about to push off and float down when he saw movement below him.

Of all the initiates to be running along the cliff face, it would of course be Gar and Bralf. They were running hard and constantly looking behind them. Ghile leaned as far out from the ledge as he dared to see their pursuers. He heard them before he saw them. A group of hunters came whooping and jeering over the rise. They were all bare chested and covered in reddish swirls. They banged their shields with clubs, closing the distance.

Ghile entertained the idea of using his powers to trip the two bullies. It would be easy enough to take a couple of stones from his pouch and hurl them at their legs. Ghile imagined the looks on their faces when they were caught and beaten into submission. They would go back in shame and have to try again next year. He reached for his pouch. A part of him truly wanted to follow through with it.

"Gar! Bralf! They are closing on you! Climb!" Ghile heard himself call.

The two swung their heads around searching for him.

"Look up!" Ghile shouted.

Bralf saw him first and he pointed him out to Gar. They both looked behind them, began to argue and finally Bralf shook his head and ran for the cliff. Gar hesitated, almost continued to run, then cursed and followed.

Ghile edged along the lip he was on until he reached the side and began the short climb to the top. The other two had their work cut out for them, but at least they would have a chance now. The hunters would have to climb as well.

Ghile didn't even need his powers to make it back to the top. There were plenty of crevices and outcroppings to use as foot and hand rests. He heaved himself over the top and rolled onto his back. The moss grew in thick clumps here, covering the stones. He massaged his aching shoulders and arms, breathing hard.

When he caught his breath, he rolled onto his stomach and peered over the edge. Both Gar and Bralf were almost to the top. A good distance below, but closing, were about half of the hunters. The others must have gone on, looking for an easier way up.

"Don't look down," one called. "It's a long drop," another added.

Ghile looked around quickly. He didn't see anyone coming. The cliff seemed to run on for quite some distance. He had never been this far into the Redwood before, but he knew he was still well up in the mountains and safe enough from everything other than the hunters. Unfortunately, he also knew these woods were well patrolled and if there were any woodsmen or fangs with them, they would know if an easier route up existed.

"Ghile! Give me a hand!" Bralf called. He'd never thought he would hear Bralf asking him for help. Ghile shrugged and reached down to pull him up. When he reached back down for Gar he only got an angry stare for his efforts. He sighed and looked around, trying to decide which way to go as Gar made the top.

"Thanks, Ghile," Bralf said, resting his hand on his knees and trying to catch his breath.

"Sure," Ghile replied. "We better be off. Some of them look to be going around," Ghile said. With that he headed away from the cliff and across the rocky, moss-covered ground. There were no trees growing along the top of the cliff and he wanted to put as much distance between himself and the hunters before they reached the top as possible.

He heard the other two following him and wondered what they were up to. He didn't have time to tell them to go away and doubted he would get more than a punch for his efforts anyway.

The three ran in silence for a while. Ghile was in the lead for some of the time, but Gar usually kept even with him. It was obvious they had about as much idea where they were going as he did. He couldn't use his powers to hide his tracks as long as they were with him. He knew they could not outrun the hunters for the entire day. Eventually they would catch up, or they would run into another group.

Renewed shouts behind him told Ghile the hunters had reached the top. There would soon be more to deal with.

The ground suddenly dropped way before them and both he and Gar almost fell, catching themselves at the last moment. They had run onto a point and hadn't realized it. Ghile searched frantically for a way down, but the cliff angled inward beneath them.

Ghile turned towards the others just in time for Gar's fist to slam into his face, knocking him to the ground.

"Damn ya to the Devourer, Ghile," Gar spat, jabbing a finger at him. "You just got us caught."

Ghile shook his head to clear it and then got up. "I didn't tell you to follow me, Gar."

Gar made to hit him again when Bralf stepped between them. "Stop it, Gar. We're going to have to fight our way out. We need him."

"Let me go, I'm tired of this little Daddy's boy." Gar tried to shake Bralf loose.

Ghile almost told Bralf to let him go. Ghile tasted blood in his mouth and it fed his anger. He was more than ready to give Gar the beating he deserved. Only the shouts of the approaching hunters stayed his hand.

Ghile looked out over the chasm. The other side was well beyond any normal jump. But, it was lower on the other side. If he was going to try it he would have to do it now. He took a few steps back.

Both Gar and Bralf seemed to realize what Ghile was about to do and stopped struggling against each other. Ghile could tell by the look on their faces what they thought. He could hear the men coming up behind them. He had to clear it all from his mind if he was going to do this.

Ghile was soaring out over nothing before he realized he had jumped. He reached over his head and pushed the thin cupped shield out above him. It caught the wind as he soared down towards the other side. He thought about letting the force shield above him go and try breaking his fall with the thicker shield, but could tell he wasn't going to make it. He was falling too fast. He felt the air rush out of him as he smacked into the opposite cliff face. The shield that had carried him across dissipated on impact and he scrambled for anything to stop his fall.

The fingers of his left hand slid into a crack and he focused all his will into those fingers, feeling his shield squeeze into the crack and slide deeper into the wall, securing him. He hung there, trying to draw air in ragged gasps.

He swung around in time to see the hunters run up beside Gar and Bralf, who still watched with eyes wide and mouths agape. The hunters all but ignored the boys, having seen him jump. They first stared down into the chasm, but on seeing him hanging from the other side, began cheering and banging their shields.

He smiled weakly and began climbing up. The full understanding of what he just did hit him and he could feel his whole body shaking. He had never felt as alive as he did just then. He kissed the side of the cliff and began laughing. Pulling himself to the top and sitting there, he waved to the other side and continued laughing.

His was still laughing to himself when the hunters grabbed Gar and Bralf and began dragging them away. Either Gar and Bralf were too stunned to put up a fight, or the hunters were too stunned to use their clubs to subdue them. Regardless, it appeared the two were going peacefully. Ghile wiped joyful tears from his eyes and looked around for where to go next.

Across the chasm, Gar suddenly thrust his leg behind one of the men holding him and brought his arm across the man's chest, tripping him. He twisted under the other hunter and was free. He turned, sprinting towards Ghile and the chasm.

Ghile jumped to his feet and waved his hands for Gar to stop. He couldn't possibly think he could make it? "No!" Ghile screamed.

He saw the look of determination on Gar's face as he took the last few strides and leaped into the air. Their eyes locked as Gar flew out across the chasm. Anger for Ghile filled his eyes, as if it was enough to will him across the gap.

It was not.

Gar's eyes still held Ghile's, but the anger was replaced with fear as he fell from sight.

28

Rite of Attrition

HILE felt nothing. He was numb. He was lined up with the other young men and women who were of age to take the Rite of Attrition. The many fires in the field outside of Lakeside cast long shadows. The faces of the spectators looked like distorted reflections. Some held torches of everflame, glowing more brightly than the regular fires. The armor of the many dwarves gathered for the rite reflected the light.

Ghile could still see Gar's face. The rest of the day had passed in a haze. He had not seen another hunter after the cliffs. He vaguely wondered if they had just left him alone after what happened. He imagined he would have been easy enough to capture. He just stumbled through the forest until he finally found himself back in the festival field and the cheering crowds outside Lakeside.

His mother had been crying and holding him, Tia still in her arms. His father had patted his shoulder and nodded his approval. "It will all be over soon and we can go home," his father had told him.

Ghile had gone through the final ceremony with the other survivors and they were now recognized as men of the Cradle. Each had then gone before the eldest druid, Mother Brambles, to be seen and potentially chosen.

Like the others, he went before her, surrounded by his family. She was lost in the song, other druids behind her, their heads bowed. He was first reminded of a shriveled fruit someone had left out under the sun. That was until her eyes opened and she pointed at him with that gnarled staff. Behind her eyes, he could see something flowing, like a river of tiny streaming lights. Ghile could feel the power coming off her in waves. Her intensity jarred him out of his self-induced stupor.

The crowd erupted with cheers and clapping. He was chosen? He was going to be a fang like his uncle? Ghile didn't know how to feel. He was both excited and terrified.

His father stepped up and solemnly, but firmly, shook his head. Of course, by the traditions his father had the right to refuse. Ghile felt an urge to push past him. He now had the courage to accept the druid's offer. He knew it would bring dishonor on his father, but this was not what stopped him. He turned and looked to his mother and Tia. How could he leave them? They had already lost Adon.

He thought of Gar and his vision was filled again with those angry, blaming eyes. Did he even deserve such an honor? In the end, the emotion filled haze that was his day settled back over him and he numbly followed his family away from the singing woman and her glowing eyes.

Ghile vaguely remembered eating something, before he heard the horns calling all those of age to the rite. So now here he stood. Waiting.

He stared down the line of waiting humans when the largest dwarf he had ever seen came into view. Every bit of the dwarf was covered in metal. The light from the bonfires danced across its armor and the huge hammer it carried in front of it.

Ghile was fascinated by the helmet on its head. It looked like a screaming dwarf, but where the helmet's mouth would have been, a wide flat face glowered out, a beard spilled forth beneath it. He lowered his head for fear the dwarf would notice him. For the first time since finding the statue, Ghile felt fear slipping back into his stomach like a fat, wet slug. Ghile heard the girl in the line beside him start to cry.

All the warnings Adon had given him about the rite came home. His mouth went dry and he couldn't swallow. He tried to take deep breaths and find his center, but they wouldn't come. He couldn't focus.

He heard that strange sound metal makes when you slide something against it and felt, rather than heard the dwarf walk towards him. He could hear ringing in his ears. Was he going to faint?

162

The ringing sound grew louder. Ghile looked up and saw the massive dwarf standing before him. The dwarf was holding his hammer before him as if he had just discovered he'd been holding a rock snake instead. The ringing sound was coming from the hammer and it started to glow. Ghile felt an intense pain rising in his chest, one that was keeping pace with the ringing and building light coming from the hammer. Ghile tried to run, but his legs wouldn't answer his plea to flee.

Somewhere in the distance he heard his mother's screams and his father shouting his name. Ghile suddenly recalled holding his mother's hand as they watched Adon being chosen by a dwarf covered in metal.

He was going to die.

"I cull thee!" the dwarf roared.

Ghile saw the hammer, its surface dancing with reflected flames, falling towards his face. He didn't have time to scream as the hammer blocked out all else. The pain in his chest consumed him.

29

Sacred Duty

INNGYR hefted the long handled hammer. Its familiar weight settled into his hands. He squeezed the relic tightly and began reciting the words of obedience all cullers learned by rote and used to reconfirm daily, their utter loyalty to Daomur.

> *Your word is law*
> *I am your vessel.*
> *I deliver your law.*
>
> *Your word is justice.*
> *I am your vessel.*
> *I deliver your justice.*
>
> *Your word is truth.*
> *I am your vessel*
> *I deliver your truth.*

In Daomur's judgment, we are preserved.

Finngyr walked into the cleared field. His armor was resplendent. He stood there looking out over the herds of humans, waiting for Daomur's judgment, huddled among the enormous bonfires.

Finngyr was born to deliver Daomur's judgment on these creatures, but even as he exulted in serving his god, he felt the itch he always did before battle. He had served on the Nordlah Plains ever since taking the oaths. The search for those who were the potential vessels of the hungering god was a war. The barbarians would fight to a man against Daomur's judgment. Every inch taken was a struggle.

Here, in this so called Cradle of the Gods, they lined up like lambs for the slaughter. Bile rose in Finngyr's mouth as he marched past the line of dwarves sent to oversee the ceremonies. He had made sure their armor shone and their weapons held keen edges.

These border guards lack discipline. They have become lazy, shepherding these humans. Every last one of them should be sent back to Daomount. One day in that holiest of the empire's mountain cities would remind these country bumpkins of the greater good they served. Bunch of squeamish beardlings, the lot of them.

Finngyr could not wait to finish this and be gone from this place. Normally, he would have waded into the thick of battle with his brother knight justices. Each armed with his ancient hammer, identical to the one Finngyr now held before him. These hammers were the most single, sacred item of his sect. It was through these blessed relics that they could identify a vessel of the Hungering God. When the hammer hummed in his grasp, he knew he had found another and he would sing Daomur's praises as he culled it from the herd. It seemed almost an insult to walk down this line of clueless humans.

The magister and his council of fat coin mongers.

He had grown so tired of their incessant whining about keeping the peace. They had asked him to just point to any he selected and they would be led back into the Bastion to be dealt with later. He would not be told how to perform his sacred duty.

He walked down the line, holding the hammer before them. They had no idea what they beheld. For a moment, one looked as if it might reach out and touch him. *Make that mistake,* Finngyr thought. As he suspected, the hammer was dormant in his grasp. Finngyr had no love of these creatures, but he would follow Daomur's law. He was not allowed to cull any who the hammer did not mark as a vessel, but in self-defense or against those who would stop him from performing his holy duty. In Daomur's name he wished they would try to stop him.

The humming caught Finngyr off guard at first. He stopped before a tall, lanky human whelp. The human's shoulders sagged and its thick dark curls still held bits of the forest from its manhood tests.

The humming grew louder.

The hammer had never made noise. He wasn't sure what was happening. The most he had ever felt was a slight thrumming. Some Justices had confided they were not always sure when they did feel it and would cull the human just to be safe.

Some of the other humans in the line looked up when the hammer began to shake in his hands. Finngyr could only stare as a light burst from it, blinding him.

The human was staring at him now, confusion and then dawning horror on his face. This was no potential vessel of the Hungering God. This was Haurtu returned to destroy them!

"I cull thee!" Finngyr roared.

He brought the hammer around his back and over in a downward stroke, all of his strength behind the blow.

Finngyr felt the impact, waited for the give of soft flesh and the familiar crunch of bone. It felt as if he had struck stone. A blinding flash and what felt like hot wind engulfed him and threw him back, the hammer flying from his grasp.

Finngyr landed hard and tightened his muscles to keep the air from being knocked from him. Crunching as much as his armor would allow, he rolled with the momentum and rose in a crouch, his side axe already in his hand.

Finngyr heard the sounds of screaming and could just make out indistinct shapes running past him. He couldn't focus his eyes. The residual image of the flash still filled his vision. He had lost his hammer. What had he hit? Surely that blow had killed the whelp?

"Dwarves! To me!" Finngyr roared.

He made his way forward. Shadows danced before him. Something pushed into him; he removed it with a swipe of his axe and was rewarded with a satisfying scream.

"Do not stand before me! I walk in Daomur's grace and all who oppose me die in his name!"

He heard the rhythmic sounds of plate sliding on chain approaching. His vision was just starting to clear when the explosions began.

30

The Rescue

IFF shielded his eyes from the flash. He didn't have time to question how Master Almoriz knew that was going to happen. He looked back in time to see both Ghile and the culler flying in opposite directions, away from each other. All this was for naught. *Useless,* he thought as he broke from the crowd and ran to where Ghile had landed in a rolling mess of limbs. *No one could have survived that blow.*

People were screaming and running in every direction. Riff reached Ghile and couldn't believe it. Not a mark. The boy's head should have been bouncing off the Horn right now. Riff didn't have time to figure it out. Ghile was writhing on the ground, clutching his chest.

"Dwarves! To me!" Riff heard from behind him. The culler wasn't as hurt as Ghile, apparently. Riff lifted Ghile up and put an arm around him to lend support.

"I'm cursed. Adon, what have you done to me?" Ghile said.

"I'm not Adon, Sheepherder. Come on, we have to go," Riff said as he pushed through the crowd. How he figured he was cursed after surviving a blow like that – blessed was more like it.

"Do not stand before me! I walk in Daomur's grace and all who oppose me die in his name!" rang out somewhere behind them.

Great, Riff thought. *Where was that diversion the Master had promised? Anytime now would be just fine, thank you.*

The entire field was suddenly illuminated as every bonfire erupted. The flames leaping up like golden red trunks to explode into roiling, fiery canopies.

The canopies came to life like so many bees and swarmed back into the bonfires that birthed them. A second explosion issued forth, throwing ash and timber in every direction.

Riff had never dreamed Master Almoriz could command that much fire. It wasn't possible. The crafty old sorcerer had been holding out on him.

People panicked in earnest now, slamming into each other in their attempt to flee. A cloud of burning ash began descending. Riff covered his face with a sleeve. He chanced a glance behind them and saw the ash forming into a thick cloud.

Now that was more like it!

170

31

His Word is Law

AD for business," Magister Obudar said. He sat there, worrying his bearded chin. He was in his audience hall again. He used to like the place. It was where he came for meals while he received reports on profits. *Not lately,* he thought.

The long, dark stone table was surrounded by his clansmen. They argued amongst each other in harsh whispers, only stopping to listen when the guards ran in to give reports. The last guard was hours overdue. Lakeside was in chaos.

Obudar slouched there, silently brooding. His lower back ached from the uncomfortable position, but the pain went with his mood. Except for his eyes, he was a statue. They moved over each of his clansmen in turn, daring one of them to return his gaze. When his clansmen had hastily shuffled in, they'd called for the gates to be shut immediately. How could he do that? Many of the humans who lived in Lakeside were still streaming in, trying to get to safety. But with them came the others. The rioters and looters. He had a responsibility to protect those who lived within the town. He understood their fear. By Daomur, he had never been more afraid in his life. But humans were not dwarves. They were not masters of their emotions.

Lakeside's human elders had already been brought before him. They asked more questions than he would have liked. Questions he did not have the answers to. Those displays of power could only come from the gods. They had never seen such power. Neither had he. He had reminded them of the precariousness of their positions if they did not help to restore the peace. Then, dismissed them from the Bastion under the protection of his guards.

He had called for a curfew when that ash cloud had descended on the festival field. Once he had the Bastion sealed and his kinsmen safe, he had sent guards out into the town to restore order. Between the displays of godly magic and that culler bludgeoning his way through the humans, he was surprised things were not worse. *Where were those druids?* He had seen Mother Brambles presiding over the manhood tests after his opening announcement. *Why hadn't she done as she was supposed to? Hadn't that young druid spoken to her? So much for their beliefs in maintaining their precious balance. If they were going to be of no use in keeping the peace, then he would have to send writs back to the capital city asking the laws that allowed their existence to be put back before the council.*

Obudar pulled on his beard. Finngyr had ignored everything he was told. *Damn him and his fervor.* Obudar again wondered if the laws concerning the knight justices and their holy purge granted too much power to the sect.

"My lord, the Sorcerer Hengon is here, as you requested," a guard announced. He and another guard had just entered, escorting the plump sorcerer behind them.

"Magister Obudar, I am here to serve," the sorcerer purred as he inclined his bald head and held out his palms with little, sausage-shaped fingers.

"Serve yourself, human!" Knight Justice Finngyr spat as he entered the magister's audience chamber. His once shining armor was covered in ash. Splatters of blood gathered in its crevices in dark splotches. He gripped his hammer tightly. It too, was sullied from its work.

"Knight Justice!" the magister shouted. "You forget your place here!" Obudar did not remember the last time he had lost his temper, but he could feel it rising now. A full squad of twelve guards followed the knight justice. They too, were covered in ash.

"Why aren't you guards patrolling the town as I ordered?" Magister Obudar demanded.

He couldn't see their faces through their visored helms, but by their body language, he could tell more than one of them would rather be anywhere else right now.

The knight justice pointed at the sorcerer. "Arrest that human. If he resists, kill him."

Hengon started backing away, looking beseechingly to the magister for help.

"Hold that order, Sergeant!" the magister said.

The guards hesitated, staring at the knight justice and the magister in turn.

Undoing its clasp and removing his helmet, the sergeant stepped forward.

Obudar had known Sergeant Montul since the day he arrived at the Cradle. Montul was a solid leader, who followed orders and never used more force than was needed to get the job done. He was as old as Obudar and hoped to finish his career with this assignment. A peaceful backwater where he could retire to long days of fishing on Crystal Lake.

The area around Montul's eyes, where his helmet allowed him to see, was an ashen mask. But, it couldn't hide the fear. "I'm sorry, Magister," Sergeant Montul said. He looked to his guards. "You heard the knight justice – take the prisoner."

"What is going on here?" Magister Obudar said.

Finngyr watched smugly as the guards seized the human. He crossed the room, removed his helmet and gauntlets, and carefully placed them on the table before the magister. Obudar watched as half dried blood and ash smeared across his accounting scrolls. "The law is being adhered to, Magister. That is what is going on here," Finngyr said. "There is a possessed vessel of Haurtu in the Cradle. Until he is captured, I am in command of all soldiers of the empire assigned here."

"But you culled him," Fjorn stated matter-of-factly from beside Obudar. At least he was keeping his emotions in check.

"It is not dead, fools! I said, an already possessed vessel! It is beyond culling. I would have captured it on the field if this human had not aided its escape."

All the blood drained from Hengon's face and he would have dropped if not for the guards holding his arms. "I have done nothing. I could not begin to control that much fire," Hengon sputtered. He looked again to Obudar. "Magister, I would never…"

The magister held up a hand. "Knight Justice, we need the soldiers to see to the safety of the citizens and goods of Lakeside."

"And there we have it," the knight justice said. "You can go guard your own warehouses, Magister. And do not bother sending for your Guard Captain. He is already under my command and gathering the other squads."

The magister lowered himself into his seat, weighing the ramifications of everything he just heard. Lakeside was to be left unguarded then. Obudar knew there was nothing he could do. The laws were quite clear. As long as a human vessel was in the Cradle, the knight justice had jurisdiction. The knight justice also now had leave to cull any human, or dwarf for that matter, who stood in his way. Obudar felt every one of his one hundred and thirty years.

Hengon sensed the shift of power. It was tangible. The sorcerer was a survivor if anything. He had a good thing catering to the dwarves and human elders of Lakeside. He was not going to let some barefoot yokel from the highlands ruin things for him. "Knight Justice, the boy you seek is Ghile of Last Hamlet. It is a small settlement in Upper Vale, in the upper most reaches of the Cradle, under the Horn," Hengon said. He normally would have held some information in reserve for a better chance to profit from it, but this dwarf frightened him. "I am not the only sorcerer in the Cradle, Knight Justice. The other is Almoriz of Whispering Rock. He and his apprentice frequent the outlying settlements."

"Is that so, human?" the knight justice said, looking at the sorcerer as if just noticing he was there.

Hengon had never liked Almoriz and his vagabond ways. He owed his old teacher nothing. They had not spoken to each other in years. Hengon did not believe even the old wizard could have controlled that much fire. It simply wasn't possible, but better the dwarves blamed Almoriz. Hengon did not want to think what would happen if he was perceived as a threat and not just a useful tool.

"Strip him bare and lock him up. We wouldn't want him using any of his tainted magic," the knight justice said as he turned back towards the table. "Then, wait for me in the entrance hall. We leave for Last Hamlet."

176

"Why do you need the entire platoon to capture one human?" Magister Obudar asked.

The knight justice donned his helmet and gauntlets, at first ignoring the question. It was only when the others began casting sidelong glances at each other that he answered in a calm, controlled voice. "That one human is a possessed vessel of Haurtu. Our doctrine says that is the first sign of the Hungering God's return. He cannot be slain by normal means; his god protects him. I must capture him and return with him to Daomount. Only the elders of my order can destroy him now."

The knight justice had their full attention now. They clung to his every word. "To add to this, he has powerful allies among the humans you have assured the empire you have full control over. If this Almoriz did, in fact, cause those magic fires and that obscuring ash cloud, then I will kill him, his apprentice, and that blubbering ball of flesh, as they are all threats to the empire," Finngyr said.

The knight justice picked up his hammer and spun on his heel. "And that is the last time I explain my actions to you simpering coin mongers." With that, Finngyr marched out, followed by the guards dragging a whimpering Hengon.

32

Sacrifice

HILE leaned against the cold damp cavern wall. He could feel it leaching warmth from him, but he welcomed the discomfort. His stomach growled again. *Good,* he thought. He should suffer. He felt it was just the beginning of what he deserved. He was cursed. He was a vessel of the Hungering God.

The pain in his chest, which he now knew came from the stone, was still there, but only a dull ache now. He considered attempting to tear into his skin and pry the black stone out with his fingers.

The stone's power had protected him from the culler's blow, yet he had suffered numerous burns from the hot coals and ash Riff had dragged him through. He had heard the others talking and knew now it had been Master Almoriz who had caused the

fire and smoke. Little else could surprise him after all
he had been through.

He had tried to escape from Riff once the searing pain in his chest had lessened to the point he
could stand on his own. Riff had guided him into the
woods, where he was met by a druid and her shieldwarden. He had been violently sick and then broke
into a stumbling run. The shieldwarden had scooped
him up and carried him like a lost lamb. He had tried
to use his powers to break free, but they would not
come to him.

They'd brought him to this cave somewhere deep
in the Redwood, where Master Almoriz and Mother
Brambles were waiting.

He screamed at them when they first tried to talk
to him. He felt a little foolish now, but at the time he
was overwhelmed by all the pain he felt about Gar
and those people he'd seen burning from the fires.
All the fears he had felt since finding the stone and
everything else had all came out of him in a stream
of tears and curses. He was especially cruel to Master Almoriz. If someone had told him he would have
called the Sorcerer of Whispering Rock a filthy, lying
murderer, he would never have believed it. But, he
had.

They had deposited him in this small side cave;
judging by the smell, the bear's lair. The bear was set
to watch him, which it now did with a bored expres-
sion. Even if the giant mountain of muscle and fur
faded off to sleep, he doubted he could squeeze past
it. It blocked all but the tiniest portion of the only

exit leading into the larger space beyond. The smell was awful.

He tried sleeping so he could enter the dream world and confront Adon on the island. But that too, did not happen. When he finally fell asleep, he had slept like the dead. He woke torn between hoping the stone might have been broken when it saved his life and fearing it was.

So, now here he sat, feeling foolish. He could see light and smelled the most delicious aromas coming from the outer cave. He could even hear voices, though they spoke in hushed tones. He was sure they were deciding what to do with him. Why had they saved him?

Of the humans he most feared in the world, a druid, a sorcerer, and a barbarian from the Nordlah Plains were at the top of the list. Though now, he would fight all three of them and this giant bear if it would mean he never had to face that dwarf again. The look on the dwarf's face when he struck him sent shivers racing across Ghile's skin. The dwarf had to be mad. Ghile thought of dwarves as being without emotion. This culler had it in buckets. No sane creature could show horror, disgust, and yet still look exultant, all at the same time. It was hard to describe, but it disturbed Ghile and he couldn't stop picturing it, like a healing scab he couldn't stop harrying.

His stomach protested again. He was so hungry. He couldn't remember the last time he had been this hungry. He didn't know what he was going to do, but at least he wouldn't have to make decisions on an empty stomach. He had sulked over his situation long enough.

He rose up and gingerly approached the resting bear. "Alright, bear. I'm not trying to escape. Please don't eat me," Ghile said.

The bear raised its head to eye level with Ghile and just stared.

"I've calmed down," Ghile called into the outer cavern.

"Let him out, Babe," he heard Mother Brambles call from behind the bear.

Babe yawned, showing a row of large teeth. They reminded Ghile of the blade his Uncle Toren carried. Shifting its bulk from side to side, Babe wiggled back out of the opening and lumbered to its feet.

"Babe?" Ghile asked. He followed behind the bear as closely as he dared.

When he could finally see around Babe, he noted this cave was not much larger than the one he had been in, about the size of a roundhouse. It had a central hearth as well, the smoke curling lazily towards the ceiling. Mother Brambles sat next to it, stirring a kettle. "That is what he was when I found him." She ladled a handful of the hearty smelling stew into a bowl. "Here. All that healing will make you hungry."

"I thought I heard the others?" Ghile asked as he moved to sit next to the hearth. He thanked her and accepted the bowl.

"I told them to eat outside. I figured you would stop punishing yourself when you smelled my stew." She motioned for him to sit.

He sat down and stared into his bowl, feeling sheepish. Ghile raised the bowl to his mouth and gingerly tested its heat.

"Suppose you know who I am?" she said.

"You are Mother Brambles. You are the chief of the druids," Ghile said. The stew was a little hot, but he was too hungry to wait.

"And you are Ghile of Last Hamlet. Son of Ecrec and Elana. You have a younger sister named Tia and you had an older brother named Adon," she stated, more than asked.

Ghile nodded. There was something about the way she said the word had. "Adon was culled," Ghile added.

"Culled or murdered?" Mother Brambles asked. She drew a small stick from the fire and lit a pipe she produced from one of the many folds in her green robes.

"I'm sorry?" Ghile said, still chewing. He stared at the ancient woman. The shaved front of her scalp was almost completely blue, the runes were so many and so close.

"You should be. But, I take it you are saying you don't understand, instead of apologizing for the way you treated the ones who saved you back at Lakeside."

Her questions had a way of feeling more like statements. "I am sorry about the way I acted," Ghile added, feeling his face warm. "I did hear you. He was culled."

182

"Why not murdered?" This time it was a question. She watched him over her pipe, her ancient eyes missing nothing. Ghile felt like a lamb who'd just spotted a wolf.

"The dwarves cull those of us who might cause the return of the Hungering God," Ghile answered as he had been taught. "It is to protect the world from his return. We are a cursed race."

"Sheep scat, the lot of it," Mother Brambles said, waving the pipe smoke away from her face along with his words.

Ghile touched his chest and felt the hard stone through his woolen tunic. How could she so easily dismiss the histories? "What I am is not sheep scat, Mother Brambles."

"And what are you, Ghile of Last Hamlet?" she said.

"I'm cursed. I'm a vessel for the Hungering God," Ghile said louder than he meant to. He had stopped eating and felt the emotions welling up in him again. He half expected her to run away screaming.

Mother Brambles continued to stare at him and puff on her pipe. "What does that feel like, then?" she asked between puffs.

"What?" Ghile couldn't believe his ears. Was she crazy? Had living all these years in a cave with a giant bear been too much for her?

"You say you are a vessel for Haurtu, the god of wisdom and learning and that you are cursed. What does that feel like?" Mother Brambles repeated.

How could she sit there so calmly? What did she mean, god of wisdom and learning? He asked as much.

"I refer to Haurtu as he was known by us, not as he is known by the dwarves," she said. She leaned back and continued to puff on her pipe. She motioned for him to continue to eat. "Eat all of that, Ghile of Last Hamlet, and I'll tell you of your people and their creator."

Ghile finished that bowl and two more, just as full. Mother Brambles told him the histories as he had never heard them. The way she told it, Haurtu was a wise god and the humans flourished under his hand. He not only created humans, but many of the other races that still existed today and some that didn't. Haurtu believed in natural selection and the survival of the fittest. She explained these concepts to Ghile. Haurtu created diversity, so the best of his creations would survive and grow wiser by surviving.

The old druid explained that Allwyn, the All Mother as Ghile knew her, was everything that was this world. She was the world itself and the air and clouds around it. She also was in a perpetual state we would most understand as dreaming.

For reasons known only to Allwyn herself, she awoke and gave birth to the Primordials. In the beginning, there were many and they were scattered across her. Some died off while others survived. Those who survived grew powerful over the ages and eventually, became something more. They could no longer die and they could create offspring as Allwyn had. And as their creator had given of herself to create them, they had to give of themselves to create. For unlike the creatures that were of the All Mother and thus were the All Mother, the Primordials were created from her, but were no longer of her.

Ghile didn't really understand this, but Mother Brambles tried to explain what the Primordials were by explaining what they were not. The Primordials were not creatures of Allwyn. They could not mate and have children, even though they seemed to have long ago chosen to be either male or female for purposes known only to them. They originally were a physical entity, but had evolved to the point they no longer needed to stay that way. But, no matter what form they chose to take, they were bound to Allwyn and existed within her. So, Ghile understood this to mean they could appear as a human or a dwarf if they wished, but could just as easily be smoke or water. The Primordials became gods.

So the Primordials who had achieved godhood created life from themselves as Allwyn had. The creatures that were created lived on Allwyn, but were not her creations. They were descended from gods, though, and thus in their own way were immortal. Ghile understood this. This was why when a person died, their soul lived on. Mother Brambles had nodded at his observation and pointed out it was the part of them that was of Allwyn; their body, that returned to her when their immortal soul left.

There were only a few Primordials who survived the long ascension to godhood. Haurtu, God of wis-

185

dom and learning. Daomur, God of law and justice. Islmur, Goddess of magic. Alyssiana, Goddess of music and art. Katriko, Goddess of love and passion. And Hideon, God of hate.

Since they were immortal, they did not need things like sleep and food. Ghile accepted that easily enough. But, they did find some form of spiritual nourishment from their followers, Mother Brambles explained. Each of the gods had taken on certain beliefs, or moral codes. When the life they had created performed those primary acts, they were nourished by it. Not like food nourishes, but more invigorated by it.

The gods thought they had found their reason for existence. They were created to thus create life and as that life went through the cycles of Allwyn they would nourish the gods with their actions.

Ghile had long ago finished his food and sat beside the fire listening to Mother Brambles. The others had come in at different stages, settling around the hearth fire, to quietly listen.

Ghile glanced at each in turn as they settled in. The young druid and her barbarian shieldwarden barely nodded at him, choosing to sit near Mother Brambles. Riff sauntered in behind Master Almoriz and sat across the hearth from Ghile. Master Almoriz stared through the flames at Ghile. He wouldn't have thought it possible to look as miserable as he felt, but the old sorcerer was succeeding. It must be those he had hurt with the flames. Riff simply dropped down and gave Ghile a confident nod, the ever-present smirk still there.

He realized as the night wore on and Mother Brambles taught him her version of the histories, he was hungry for the knowledge. He wanted to know. He said as much to Mother Brambles and she pointed out this was only natural. He was human and thus descended from Haurtu, God of learning and wisdom. *Haurtu the Hungerer,* Ghile thought to himself.

It was this very hunger that lead to Haurtu's exile. He came to the belief that the other gods were wrong, this was not their purpose. He too was sustained by the worship of his creations, but felt the gods had stopped evolving. Everything that lived as part of Allwyn struggled to survive and through that struggle, grew. Haurtu felt the gods were stagnant. They were meant to evolve. But to what end? Haurtu thought on this for a very long time, but eventually came to the conclusion that the All Mother really wanted an All Father. That was why she had awoken and created them separate from her. She wanted an All Father to join her in her eternal dream, thus completing her. Did not all her creations have a male and female aspect?

Haurtu acted on his discovery and attacked his fellow gods. At first, the gods did not understand what he was doing. They could not be destroyed. They were eternal. But Haurtu also knew this and had never intended on destroying them. Upon defeating them, he consumed them.

Here Ghile was confused again. Haurtu ate them? Mother Brambles replied it was more like when moss absorbs water. Haurtu defeated them and then absorbed them into his being. The two became one. Ghile didn't understand where the other gods went once absorbed by Haurtu, but no other explanations Mother Brambles tried to give made any sense to him.

One by one, Haurtu challenged and consumed the other gods. First Alyssiana, then Katriko. But, this war was not only fought between the gods. Their creations also warred. Humans fought against the other races of Allwyn, just as their god fought against the creators of the other Races. It is said even the other creations of Haurtu fought alongside the humans. Of these races, Mother Brambles only knew of the goblins and vargan as races that still existed today.

Hideon knew they must come together and attack Haurtu. But with each god Haurtu defeated, he grew in power as did those who worshiped him. Hideon had a plan. The remaining gods, Daomur, Islmur, and Hideon confronted Haurtu. Hideon battled Haurtu and in the ensuing battle, Hideon was consumed. But Hideon's sacrifice allowed the last two to trap Haurtu. Islmur used her magic to open a doorway to the space outside Allwyn, a place not in any place, but more between. There, Haurtu was banished. Daomur bound the door with his laws and decreed only Haurtu could free himself. The perfect trap, or so the gods thought.

Ghile thought about what he had been taught about the Hungering God. The version he had learned taught that Haurtu had gone mad and consumed the other gods. But Mother Brambles suggested Daomur, Islmur and Hideon had defeated him and exiled him from Allwyn.

Mother Brambles shared how after Haurtu's banishment, the gods returned to their docile existence of being nourished by their followers. The humans were decimated and those that survived dispersed. The other races of Haurtu were either annihilated, or such a small number remained that they skulked off into the ruins and wilds of Allwyn.

They thought it was over. But Haurtu was wise, and discovered a way over time to reach back into Allwyn and seed himself into his creations, and through them, free himself from his prison.

Upon discovering this, Daomur charged his most abundant surviving race, the dwarves along with Islmur's, the elves, to remove Haurtu's races from the face of Allwyn for good. Ghile knew of this time. It was called the Great Purge.

Ghile told Mother Brambles this was when the first druids had sung to the All Mother. Mother Brambles agreed, but said they were not druids then, but the surviving priestesses of Haurtu. With the banishment of their god, they had lost the power that comes to those who make their life's work serving their god's tenants.

They knew no other god would listen to them so they prayed to Allwyn for mercy, the only thing they thought could save them. Many had tried praying to the Mother of the Gods in the past. Even the gods had tried to awaken her to learn from her, but none had ever succeeded.

But it was in this hour of need, when the human race was almost at the point of extinction, that a female priestess of Haurtu finally heard the All Mother's Dream Song and for the second time since all creation, awoke her.

Allwyn rose to the defense of Haurtu's offspring and commanded the gods to end the purge. Daomur and Islmur pleaded with Allwyn and they came to an accord. If the purge was ended, the remaining gods could do only what was needed to keep Haurtu imprisoned. Mother Brambles pointed out that the All Mother would not answer the remaining gods whether what Haurtu had done was right or wrong. The concept seemed foreign to her. Allwyn then returned to her dreaming.

So, Daomur passed laws down to his followers that they were to shepherd the humans and cull those Haurtu might use to enact his return. He further restricted them from things that were sacred to Daomur to show his disfavor. The working of stone and the creation of metal were to be acts that honored him and thus forbidden to the races of Haurtu.

Islmur also passed tenets to the elves, forbidding them from sharing the knowledge of learned magic with the surviving races of Haurtu. They shared the art of imbuing magic into objects with the dwarves before they retreated to their goddess's sacred places in the Deepwood. It is said Islmur lives among them and nurtures them still.

But, all was not lost for those descended from Haurtu. Those races who had lost their god were not completely forsaken. Certain ones, for some unexplained reason, always females, could now hear the Dream Song. They could listen and learn the way she wanted her children to live. This was the birth of the druids.

Ghile asked of sorcerers. Mother Brambles was not certain why, but a very select few human males had the innate ability of magic buried deep within them. Some say they are descendants of generations of powerful wizards who had survived the Great Purge and still held the magic they had once practiced deep within them. But, she did not know the truth of it.

Those that showed the gift were but shadows of their ancestors and were but mere tinkerers in comparison. They were not considered threats by the other races.

Ghile asked how what Master Almoriz had done with the fires could not be seen as a threat?

"It would appear the presence of a stonechosen augments our magic," Master Almoriz said. The guilt in his voice called to Ghile's own.

Mother Brambles patted his knee. "You did not know, Almoriz."

"What does that mean? I don't understand," Ghile asked.

"It means you are my new best friend," Riff said.

The others had eventually sought their furs for some much needed rest. Ghile lay there near the hearth, staring at the flames. They seemed to trust he would not try to run again. Babe seemed happy to have his den back and the rumblings of his snores echoed off the cave's uneven walls.

What did this all mean for him? He was a chosen of Haurtu. An instrument in his return. How? Did he want the banished god freed? He wasn't sure, but he definitely didn't want to die.

Sometime during the morning, he felt his powers slowly return. He entertained the idea of sharing his dream teachings with Mother Brambles and the others, then reconsidered. Somehow it didn't seem the time. He knew more than he had, but he still didn't know what he was going to do.

He thought about his family and knew they would be in danger because of him. He wished he could speak with his uncle. He was always there when Ghile needed advice. It was then that he realized Uncle Toren had never arrived in Lakeside for the summer festival or his first Rite of Attrition. Nothing could have kept him from being there for Ghile. Something must have happened to him on the Horn. Ghile needed to find out what.

33

Decisions

HILE wished he had more time. He kept pacing back and forth in front of Mother Bramble's cave. Riff knelt near the entrance, his back against the stone cliff, silently watching.

Ghile knew his family was in danger. He was sure the dwarves were already looking for him and the first place they would go was Last Hamlet. He hoped his father was thinking the same thing and took the family to safety.

His very existence was hurting those around him. Gar was dead because he had tried to do what he had seen Ghile do. He had no way of knowing Ghile had used his new powers to make that jump. Ghile knew he hadn't forced Gar to jump, but he bore the guilt all the same.

What would the dwarves do when they didn't find him in Last Hamlet? The look on the culler's face left little doubt in Ghile's mind. He had to go to Last Hamlet and stop the dwarves from hurting anyone else because of him.

But what to do about his new companions? They were only interested in getting him as far away from the Cradle as possible. He was too special to risk now, they had said.

Damn the gods, he hadn't asked for any of this.

He had even thought of taking his own life. It was the one way he felt he could make sure those he loved would be safe. But, he hated to admit to himself he was afraid to try. He remembered the way Adon had described the souls of his race floating in some kind of dreaming limbo. Could he commit himself to that? He had committed Gar to it already. Those people who died in the ash and fire. They were now there as well. Waiting.

What about his race? He had the chance to free the god that created them and in doing so, free the souls trapped in that limbo and allow them to re-enter the cycle. Be reborn to live new lives. If he went with his new protectors, he could help free his people from the dwarves. Not free like the barbarians, under constant attack, but free and equal. They would have their god back. They could call on him for aid.

But would he listen? In freeing Haurtu, would he just attack the gods again? Mother Brambles had described the war that was fought on Allwyn while the

194

gods battled. Would freeing Haurtu bring about such a war?

Ghile could feel the panic crawling up from deep inside him. He had only just become a man. He still felt very much a boy. Why was he having to make these kinds of decisions? He told himself to remain calm, stopped pacing and slowed his breathing.

Think, Ghile. There is nothing for it now. You have to think.

Right. If they wanted him to flee the Cradle, they would have to help him first. He wanted to find his uncle and make sure he was all right, and talk with him. He also wanted the people of Last Hamlet safe from any persecution. If they helped him do those things, then he would go with them.

As for his role in freeing Haurtu, he was not sure yet. He knew he wanted the souls of his race to return to the cycle. He would do it for that alone, but he did not want to bring a mad god back into Allwyn so he could start another war. He would have to find some way to free Haurtu and convince him not to pursue his quest to become the All Father. Ghile laughed at himself. *How do you expect to do that, Sheepherder?*

"Alright, Riff," Ghile said. "I'll do it. I'll be their key. But, they are going to have to do something for me first."

Riff raised an eyebrow and then issued a low whistle. "Well, look who has some bass in his voice." Riff jumped to his feet, dusting off his hands. "Let's get in there and tell them. I wanna see the look on their faces," Riff said.

Ghile nodded and headed into the cave, with a grinning Riff following close behind.

∧

They made their way along the base of the Horn, following Two Elks. The swollen clouds hung low in the sky like a blanket piled against the mountains. A steady rain fell and Ghile had given up trying to remain dry hours ago.

The barbarian had never been on the Horn, but Two Elks assured them he could find Ghile's uncle if he was somewhere on the mountain. They had only taken the time they needed to pack provisions and the extra protection from the elements they were going to need if they had to stay too long on the icy and treacherous peak.

Master Almoriz was on his way to Last Hamlet. He had promised to warn them of the danger they were in and convince them to leave the Hamlet, or if he was too late, help defend them. He had said he had nothing to lose. He had almost looked eager at the prospect.

Ghile had wanted Mother Brambles to go with him, but she had refused. She had not been surprised when Ghile and Riff had returned to give Ghile's demands, much to Riff's disappointment. She had been in the midst of preparing to leave when they had entered. She said she had sung on all this and she was supposed to return to Lakeside. Though she would not say what she was going to do when she got there.

Ghile didn't understand what she meant when she said she had sung on something, but he understood enough to know she knew what needed to be done. Could the old druid look into the future? It wouldn't be the biggest surprise he'd discovered recently.

Two Elks motioned for them to stop as he examined the ground. Gaidel moved up beside him and they spoke softly to each other. Gaidel finally nodded and Two Elks pulled his large stone axe from its harness and started up a steep incline at a fast trot.

"He has found a well-used trail and is going to scout ahead. Time is against us, the ground is soft and the rain is washing away the tracks," Gaidel said as she walked back to Riff and Ghile.

"So, you and the barbarian," Riff began, flashing that annoying smile at Gaidel. Ghile moaned.

"Do you understand what is at stake here, Sorcerer?" Gaidel said, thin lipped.

Riff glanced around and placed his hand near his mouth to whisper. "What? Is Two Elks the jealous type?"

"We should have already left the Cradle. The longer this boy makes us remain here, chasing down his family members, the more we risk everything!"

"Boy?" Ghile said.

Riff made a serious face and nodded. "Too bad you aren't the one who gets to make those important decisions, isn't it, Druid?"

"I passed my manhood test!" Ghile grumbled, though no one seemed to be paying him any attention.

"Why are you even here, Sorcerer? We don't need you. We can sharpen our own weapons and light our own fires. Isn't there a pot in some village you could be mending?" Gaidel said.

"You are not that much older than I am," Ghile said.

Riff put an arm around Ghile's shoulder, grinning wider.

"Again, not your decision, Druid. You don't even know what I'm capable of with Ghile around. I might surprise you."

Gaidel gave them both a withering stare and turned to follow Two Elks.

"I am not a boy!" Ghile called after her.

"This is going to be fun," Riff said, patting Ghile's shoulder. He followed after Gaidel.

Ghile wasn't so sure.

34

Best Laid Plans

o! No! No!" Muk said with each stamp of his feet.

Bloody Maw watched quietly as Muk stomped in a circle, only reacting when one of the goblin's feet came down in a puddle, sending water flying. Once the goblin had released enough frustration, Muk crawled back to the edge and peered over again. Even with the heavy gray clouds shielding his sensitive eyes from the sun, Muk still had to squint. He could just make out the four figures making their way along one of the lower trails.

Muk could sense one of them was the boy who had his other stone. This was not how he had planned it. The boy was supposed to be alone. Muk had ridden Bloody Maw down the mountain last night and used his powers to call one of the scrawny mutts the humans used to protect their lair. He had given it the knife of the human he had captured and then sent it back into the village with an image of the boy in its mind. He had almost killed the creature when he saw it expected a small tribute of food for its services. It had received a good kick instead.

The boy was supposed to see the knife and then come alone. This would not do. Muk sat down next to Bloody Maw and used the worg to shield him from the rain. He had to think of another plan.

He had to keep the others busy while he lured the boy away. He could send the pack at them, but he wanted as much help as he could get to defeat the boy. It had a stone like his and Muk wasn't going to take any chances.

What he needed was more creatures. *That was it,* thought Muk. He needed more help. He closed his eyes and concentrated as the dream teacher had taught him. He took the breaths that were important to help the magic work. He immediately sensed Bloody Maw's mind. The worg was hungry and bored as usual and wanted to hunt something down to torment and then devour. Muk moved his mind out farther, ignoring Bloody Maw's thoughts. He kept reaching. He found many small minds of creatures who lived on the ugly mountain. But none of them would do. He reached deeper into the stone. There. Yes, there was a mind.

This creature was big. Very big. Muk hesitated. He had never tried controlling something this big. It was far away and Muk knew his power waned as the distance between him and his thralls grew. If he did try and use this creature, he could not risk getting close to it. He had not come this far just to be eaten on this ugly mountain.

Muk could sense it slumbered and tried to wake it. It resisted, it was not time to wake. It was not cold enough yet. This creature hibernated until it was colder. Muk became annoyed and reached out and hurt it in its mind. Muk was master and Muk needed the big ugly thing to wake up and go eat the humans on the mountain. The creature stirred. It had tasted human flesh before and it had not fed since it had crawled deep into the mountain to sleep. *Go*, Muk pushed at the creature's mind. *Go and eat the humans. All, but the tall skinny one. He tastes bad. Him you do not eat. He is mine.* Muk felt the creature yawn, and start crawling its way to the surface.

Opening his eyes Muk took a moment to clear his head and regain his strength. He then scurried up onto Bloody Maw's back. He straightened the captured human's bow, which he had hung over his shoulder. He thought Bloody Maw into movement. He had to get down there and get into place. He hoped this worked. He would have to get closer to his creature to be sure it did not eat the boy. He had another plan.

35

On the Edge

HILE covered his face with his hand and tried to see through the rain pelting the Horn. Someone was watching them. He couldn't see anyone as he looked up the uneven ledges and steep rises of the mountain side, he could just feel it on the nape of his neck. There was someone or something out there.

"Daughter Gaidel, we are being watched," Ghile called.

The druid didn't stop walking, but hazarded a look up above them and then behind. "I do not see anything. Are you sure? Two Elks hasn't given any sign," Gaidel said.

Just as she finished speaking, Two Elks came sprinting back along the thin ledge they had been following, water splashing up from the rivulets of rain zigzagging down its surface.

Ghile watched in horror at the barbarian's perilous strides. The mud-slick trail clung to the mountain on one side and opened into emptiness on the other.

Riff came up behind Ghile, his hood pulled far over his face. "Why is the fool running?"

Riff quickly had his answer. A creature came into view following closely behind Two Elks. It was huge, easily twice as long as the barbarian was tall. At least eight legs worked together to propel it forward and help it cling to the mountain's uneven surface. Its leathery skin was pure white, from its long, fang-filled maw to its lashing tail. All the stories Uncle Toren had told Ghile of the dreaded frost wyrms came rushing back.

Those long-taloned claws looked as if they would be equally good at rending flesh or anchoring the monster onto the mountainside. It closed the distance between itself and Two Elks in a sudden burst of speed. Ghile heard a cry of warning before he realized it had come from him.

Two Elks had been expecting the attack – the agile barbarian spun, shield in the lead, and reflected the frost wyrm's bite and front-sweeping claw. He continued the turn and brought his stone axe arcing through, catching the wyrm on the shoulder. The stone blade did little damage to its hide from what Ghile could see.

Ghile didn't understand why this thing was awake. It should still be asleep. For whatever reason, this one was awake and looked none too happy about it.

"Back, go back!" Two Elks shouted as he followed his spin through and kept running along the ledge.

Ghile had little time to marvel at the barbarian's balance as he turned to do as he was told. He heard Gaidel right behind him. He had to push Riff, who was in the middle of digging in one of his many pouches.

"No time, Riff. Go!" Ghile screamed as he pushed against the sorcerer.

Riff turned and began moving as fast as he could back along the ledge. Ghile remembered the stories of how agile the frost wyrms were and knew they couldn't outrun the beast.

Ghile heard a high pitched, undulating hiss from much closer behind him. It sounded like it was right over his shoulder and he screamed when Gaidel pushed him in the back, urging him on.

Ghile could see Riff had reached a portion of the trail where the ledge widened out to form a long flat landing. Ghile remembered passing it and thinking how relieved he was, not to have to be reminded how steep the drop was.

Riff moved to the center of the landing and started digging into his pouches again. Ghile followed along the cliff face as far from the ledge as possible.

Two Elks moved to take a position beside Gaidel.

"Keep moving back, Ghile. As far back as you can," Gaidel said as she turned and took a defensive stance, her staff before her.

Ghile hastened to do just that, but felt his feet get ahead of themselves, like they often did, and fell hard against the wall. He scratched both palms trying to stay upright but only managed to get more twisted. He collapsed in a heap.

Ghile saw Gaidel start to sway and heard the singing. He could only watch as the frost wyrm landed before the two of them and swept its huge tail across the landing. Two Elks only managed to get his shield in front of Gaidel as the tail sent both of them flying past Ghile to land near Riff, who had finally managed to produce an everflame from his pouch.

There was nothing between Ghile and the wyrm. Ghile brought his hands before him. He had to relax and get his force shield up. The frost wyrm crawled toward him with incredible speed. He lost all focus when he saw its mouth open and heard another of those terrifying hisses pour forth. He shielded his face as the wyrm charged past him towards his companions.

What was happening?

Ghile watched in shock as he saw the clawed legs scuttle by one after the other. The creature acted as if he wasn't even there.

Ghile scrambled to his feet just as a gout of flame shot out of Riff's hand, scoring several burns along the wyrm's head and neck. Frost wyrms feared few things more than fire. The taloned legs seem to switch direction of their own accord, trying to get their owner's body away from the new threat.

Riff's face danced in the glow of the flames as his spell continued to billow out along the beast's flank.

"Oh, Ghile, you beautiful stonechosen, you!" Riff's laughter mixed with the wyrm's snarls.

Riff had bought Gaidel and Two Elks enough time to get back to their feet. The frost wyrm stalked along the edge of the landing, cautiously circling the three of them. Ghile wasn't sure why it hadn't killed him. He had not brought his shield up. But, the creature was not concentrating on him now. He tried to think how he could help in this battle. He could feel his heart trying to beat its way out of his chest and his blood thudding in his ears. The idea of running came to him, but he pushed it away. He had to help.

Something grazed the back of his shoulder and flew past his face, leaving behind a stinging pain. Ghile saw an arrow reflect off the cliff face and fly off into empty space.

He threw his hand onto his back and felt a warm wetness. He knew if he looked at his palm he was going to see his own blood. Instead, he looked back up the trail they had just fled down and all thoughts of the frost wyrm and his wound vanished.

It was not the large wolf that surprised him. True, it was the biggest wolf he had ever seen, but that was not what had his attention. The small green creature clinging to its back wasn't what locked his gaze. He even recognized the bow in the creature's grasp as his Uncle Toren's and somewhere it registered in Ghile's mind it was this goblin who had just shot him with an arrow from his own uncle's bow. All this his mind took in an instant, but it was the small, raised stone-like welt in the Goblin's chest that captured Ghile's focus.

The Goblin raised the bow and shouted at Ghile in a language he didn't understand. But Ghile could hear the creature's words in his head even as he heard the unintelligible speech in his ears.

"You know this bow! I have him, human mutt! I have the man who looks like you! I go to kill him now!" The little goblin screamed. Then the wolf turned and bounded up the trail.

Ghile found himself following. That goblin had a stone just like his. It was stonechosen, like he was. Ghile felt a desire like none he had ever felt before, more than any hunger or thirst. He wanted that stone. He needed it.

He knew now that was the presence he had felt watching him. He moved along the ledge, all fear of falling forgotten. He couldn't see the goblin or the huge wolf it was riding, but it didn't matter. He could feel where it was now. Somewhere in his mind a part of him wondered what he was going to do when he caught up to them. But it was barely a whisper compared to the desire to have that stone.

"Ghile, stop! Where are you going?" Riff shouted. He could see Ghile running up the muddy ledge. He would have thought the sheepherder was fleeing from the wyrm had he not seen the worg with the lowland goblin on its back.

*What were those things doing in the Cradle? More to
the point, why was Ghile chasing them? Had he finally
lost his mind? The kid was barely a match for the goblin
alone.*

Riff reached into the everflame and pulled forth another gout of flame and threw it into the air between
him and the frost wyrm. He berated himself again for
not being able to find which pocket he had put it in
sooner, but these things happened. The flame diminished noticeably, the farther Ghile ran up the trail.
"Nice, Ghile, real nice."

The wyrm was keeping its distance for the time
being, but Riff knew things weren't going to stay that
way. The barbarian and the druid were finally back
on their feet. Two Elks didn't look any worse for having been slapped silly, but Gaidel still seemed a bit
unsteady.

Well, she'd better get her senses about her and fast.
"Alright, you two. How about some help?" Riff said.

It looked like the wyrm was figuring out the flames
were now more of a nuisance than a threat. Riff
wished Ghile hadn't run off. He wished he had practiced this spell more. He could hear Master Almoriz
now. "There will come a time you will wish you had
practiced more, Apprentice, but then it will be too
late." How was he supposed to know he was going to
be squaring off against a frost wyrm on the side of
the Horn in the middle of summer? This one would
have been tough for anybody to call.

Two Elks banged his stone axe against his shield and roared at the wyrm as he charged towards it. Riff had to admit, the barbarian wasn't easily scared.

The wyrm lunged forward and grabbed hold of the barbarian's shield with its two front limbs, its head reaching over the shield, jaws snapping. Two Elks held on tight to his shield and swung his great axe at the limbs, all the while trying to keep away from those snapping jaws.

Riff moved down the creature's flank and threw another gout of the diminished flame against its hide. He fell flat, barely dodging the creature's tail as it whipped through the space where his head had just been.

Gaidel's clear voice echoed off the cliff side as she swayed to some unheard music. Riff knew this was how she asked the All Mother for help. He hoped the old girl was listening. They were going to need all the help they could get.

36

The Cave

HE rain-soaked ground gave way under Ghile's hand, mud squishing between his fingers as he climbed the steep embankment in pursuit of the stone. He could feel its pull growing stronger. As he felt his way through the rain, he wondered where it had come upon a stone. Who had the stone allowed the goblin to visit in his dreams? What secrets of the old ones had it been taught? All these thoughts warred inside Ghile's head as he climbed.

He pulled himself up over another ledge. His hair hung wet, clinging to his face. He tried to shake his vision clear, tossing his head like a dog, since his hands were covered with mud. He finally decided it didn't matter and used his hands to clear his eyes.

He found himself on a wide ledge. He turned and looked back. He could no longer see the others, though he could still hear the sounds of battle somewhere below him. What he could see though, far off in the valley, was Last Hamlet. The sheets of rain made it look like he was looking at a village on the bottom of a lake. Ghile hoped Master Almoriz had gotten there in time to lead his family to safety.

A part of him still worried over his family. But, the majority was focused on the stone he had seen in the goblin's chest. He knew this desire was unreasonable. Why would he want another stone? The first one had torn into his flesh and crawled its way under his skin to burn itself into his very bone. Why would he want to experience that again? If he had any sense, he would be running from the thing, not risking his very life to possess it. But, here he was. Some part of him had to have it, hungered for it.

Across the ledge, partly hidden by an outcropping of rock, Ghile could see the mouth of one of the many caves of the Horn. The pull of the other stone was coming from there. Ghile didn't hesitate, he leaned forward and began to run across the ledge, straight into the dark, yawning maw.

Ghile couldn't see anything, his eyes slowly adjusting to the darkness, but his sense of smell was immediate. He was assaulted by the raw mix of musk and urine. He forced down the reflex to gag and covered his nose with a wet sleeve. The sounds of something scraping across stone came from somewhere up ahead. His eyes adjusted enough for him to make out three dark shadows skulking towards him.

He wished he could see and then, as if something had been waiting to answer his request, he could. Everything came into focus. He stood in a short entryway to a much larger cavern. Three giant wolves, like the one the goblin had been riding, were creeping silently towards him. Farther back in the cavern, he could see the goblin next to the wolf it had been riding. They were both against the far wall, waiting for the other wolves to strike.

The goblin hopped from one stubby leg to the other. The large wolf paced nearby. As it moved, it revealed a bound man lying on the ground behind it. Ghile recognized Uncle Toren.

He realized his uncle couldn't see him in the dim light. Ghile didn't understand why he could see so clearly. It must be another gift of a stonechosen. He didn't have time to mull it over. Right now, he had to deal with the three giant wolves.

Ghile only had a few more seconds before they would be on him. He was alone and in a cave with four enormous wolves and a goblin which likely had powers to match his own. Had this been the Ghile of a few months ago, he would have run from this cave screaming. The Ghile here, now, knew he had to even these odds. He took a deep centering breath and focused his mind.

His force shield would be helpful, but he needed to take the attack to them. He reached down and pulled the pouch containing his practice stones from his belt. He poured them into his outstretched hand even as the first wolf leaped towards him.

All four stones shot out toward the creature in quick succession. Ghile had always practiced on things far away and had never really thought of how fast he could actually push the stones away from him. He was surprised when the stones didn't bounce off the leaping wolf, but tore into its hide with four small explosions of blood and fur. Ghile fell to the side to avoid the wolf's corpse as it thudded to the ground beside him. He had barely come to the realization he had just killed one when the other two attacked.

Instinct alone was all that saved him as he brought his force shield up before the leaping wolf knocked him to the ground and tried to bite down on his throat. He felt the strength of its jaws as the force shield strained under the pressure. The wolf's flexing maw was only inches from his face. Its saliva was smeared across the shield. The wolf tried to twist and rip at the unseen force stopping it from reaching its prey.

Ghile didn't have any more stones and had to deal with this one quickly. The shield strained in his mind and he almost lost focus. Ghile thought of Gar's eyes as he fell and wondered if his eyes now held the same look of shock and fear. The thought of Gar reminded him of his jump and how he had clung to the cliff side. Ghile concentrated the force shield between the wolf's jaws. He felt it filling the gap and began extending it deeper into the creature's throat.

A sharp pain in his ankle almost caused him to lose the shield for a second time. By focusing on a small part of the shield and molding it, the whole shield was shrinking. The other wolf had locked its jaws on his foot and was savaging it. Ghile had never experienced such pain. He felt his flesh give and the animal's teeth scrape against bone.

Ghile cried out, but somehow manage to keep focus on the force shield. He knew he had to hurry and finish the first wolf. He felt waves of nausea wash over him as the other wolf continued to tear at his leg, trying to pull him away from its pack mate. If Ghile had not used his force shield to protect his neck, the two would have ripped him apart. As it was, if he didn't do something and fast, he feared he was going to lose his foot.

He focused his mind and pushed deeper into the throat of the first wolf. He felt resistance and concentrated on growing the shield. The pain in his leg seemed to shift away from the forefront of his consciousness as he focused his will on his shield. Inch by trembling inch he forced it to expand.

All resistance to the shield vanished as the wolf's lower jaw dislocated with a loud snap. The wolf fell to the ground writhing in pain and rubbing at its muzzle with its paws.

Suddenly, Ghile was sliding along the uneven stone floor. The wolf that had his foot and ankle no longer struggled against the pull of the other and was dragging him deeper into the cave. Ghile closed his eyes and focused on his wounded ankle. He imagined the force shield wrapped around his ankle like a bandage and expanded it out. Another satisfying crack echoed through the cavern as the other wolf's jaw snapped. It too fell back, writhing on the floor.

"Kill him, Bloody Maw! Kill Him!" Ghile felt the words in his head even as he heard the sharp guttural language. The goblin jumped up and down frantically, pointing at him.

Ghile pushed himself up and tried to stand. The pain in his leg was white hot. Black spots danced across his eyes as his body threatened to shut down and escape.

He fell back to the ground, clutching his ankle in both hands. Blood flowed through his fingers as he tried to put pressure on the wound. He tried to focus and create another shield, but the image slipped from his thoughts on a river of agony. He searched the floor near him for anything he could try and force throw at the approaching wolf.

Blood Maw stalked towards him, a deep growl accompanying each padded step. It followed his eyes as he searched the floor. Bloody Maw looked from Ghile's wounded ankle to the barren floor around him and appeared to give its massive shoulders a shrug. It quirked its ears and then made an odd half step to the left, as if getting out of the way of something.

Past the immense wolf, he saw the goblin nock an arrow. Ghile lay in the middle of the cavern, gripping his ankle, waiting for death.

Gaidel tried to sing with the All Mother's song as the serpentine predator went rushing past her. She was the mountainside. Thousands of tiny rain drops slapped her skin. Wind pushed against her, forever taking a little bit of her with it as it wore her away. She was ancient. Gaidel had to concentrate. "I am Gaidel," she repeated to herself. She felt her companions and the frost wyrm move across her. Gaidel heard something wrong in the wyrm's song. She knew now it had been awakened unnaturally from its hibernation and was both angry and hungry. The wyrm's song rang discordant. She sang with the frost wyrm, tried to guide its song away from attacking them. Too much anger. She felt its hunger and her stomach growled. Her mouth watered for the taste of flesh.

Gaidel guided her song away from the wyrm's discordant rhythm and sang with the nearby stones. If she could just make them listen.

"Go save the boy!" Two Elks shouted at Riff, as he struggled to free his shield from the wyrm's grasp.

Riff shot another gout of flame onto the wyrm and shook his head. "Because you have this situation so well in hand? I think not," Riff said.

He was worried for Ghile, but he knew his own chances for survival rested with these two in taking down this wyrm and not with Ghile, the goblin, and its worg mount.

Suddenly, Riff's feet lurched out from under him and he fell back against the side of the cliff. He scrambled to stay away from the edge. He heard a moist, sucking sound as the stone he had been standing on pulled itself from the mud. He slid along the wall and protected his everflame as other stones mimicked their companion and also tore themselves free. They began sliding and tumbling of their own accord towards the frost wyrm.

Not bad, Riff had to admit. He watched Gaidel sway, her eyes closed, lost in the song.

The stones slammed against the wyrm's legs and side, causing it to release its grip on Two Elks and struggle to remain upright. Its many legs scrambled for purchase, but each time it found a surface to cling to and right itself, another stone crashed into the securing limb pushing the beast closer to the edge.

Riff crawled to his feet and moved forward, ready to throw another flame.

"The boy, witch!" Two elks shouted.

It took a moment for Riff to realize the barbarian meant him. "Witch?" Riff repeated.

Two Elks regained his balance and sprang to his feet. Riff watched the barbarian drive his shield into the head of the frost wyrm and set about its long neck and shoulder with his great axe. The stone blade had long since lost its edge against the wyrm's thick hide. But, Two Elks was now using it more like a club. Riff had a brief vision of Two Elks coming at him with that shield and axe, and felt his chances of survival shift suddenly with Ghile.

217

"If Ghile is hurt, I bring pain to you!" Two Elks shouted again.

"Hang on, Ghile. Help is on the way!" Riff called.

37

Inner Strength

LOODY Maw dug in deep with its thick claws and savagely snapped its jaws down again and again, but Ghile's thin shield held off its attacks. When Bloody Maw finally closed the distance with a mighty leap, Ghile had found the strength of will to bring a small force shield into existence between them. But the giant wolf was immensely strong, and with each attack, the shield weakened and Ghile was shoved further back. He gritted his teeth through the throbbing pain in his ankle. He felt another cut open along his back as he was forced across the uneven floor.

He waited for the twang of the bow string and the pain that would surely follow. He couldn't risk a glance towards the goblin, since Bloody Maw was testing the size of his shield by circling and coming at him from different angles. Ghile had tried putting the wolf between him and the goblin, but his ankle wouldn't allow it.

Bloody Maw's growls and barks echoed throughout the cavern as it repeatedly threw itself against Ghile's force shield. Ghile felt his back slam against stone. He shook small dancing lights from his vision. He had been forced against the cavern wall. His own force shield slammed into him as Bloody Maw continued its assault. The air was forced out of him with each impact. He could feel the shield weakening.

Bloody Maw let out a painful yelp and sprung back off Ghile. Ghile shook his head and gulped in air as he took advantage of the lull in the attack. Across the room, the goblin was repeatedly smashing Uncle Toren, who had apparently thrown his bound body against it, making the shot aimed for Ghile go awry and hit Bloody Maw. Ghile cheered for his uncle, and felt the strength to fight bolstered by his example. "I'm here, Uncle. Fight on!" Ghile screamed.

Bloody Maw tore the arrow from its flank with its jaws and growled at Ghile, its thick hackles rising. It tensed its muscles for another attack.

Ghile looked about. He was going to be crushed between his own force shield and the wall and there was nothing he could do to stop it.

"For the Cradle!" He heard his uncle shout. Ghile braced his shield and took one last look towards his uncle. The goblin had finally got back to its feet and was drawing a knife from its belt. Uncle Toren struggled against his bonds, striking out with his feet in a last attempt to keep the creature at bay. It seemed both he and his uncle were destined to die in this cave.

Ghile was blinded as a gout of flame flew over Bloody Maw.

"Bad dog!" Riff called out as he followed the gout with a second and then a third blast.

The smell of burnt hair and sizzled flesh filled Ghile's nostrils. He gratefully released his concentration on his force shield and felt the heat of Riff's attack wash over him. Bloody Maw thrashed against the flames.

"Don't die on me yet, Sheepherder!" Riff called out, laughing as he set another burst of flames onto the thrashing wolf. Riff appeared to be reveling in his new found powers. Ghile watched the light of the flames dance across Riff's face.

Ghile was not sure if it was the pain or loss of blood, but in that moment he could see Master Almoriz's face as he let loose his fire spell back at the festival. The realization of the power his presence released within the two sorcerers washed over him. The sounds of the wolf's howls were replaced with the screams of the people at the festival.

Ghile had to get away. He used his arm as a brace and tried to rise, but the small outcropping of wall he was using as support gave under his weight and he fell to the floor among pieces of falling stone. He puzzled over the small jagged rock for a moment before he remembered where he was. "Thank the All Mother," Ghile gasped, as he grabbed the rock and held his hand towards the goblin. With a mental push the rock shot across the distance.

The goblin had finally grabbed Toren's bound legs and was raising its blade for a killing blow. Ghile's rock slammed against the side of its head. There was a dazzling flash of white from the soulstone in the goblin's chest, and from where Ghile's projectile should have impacted. The goblin flew away from Ghile's uncle, its stolen blade clattering across the hard stone floor.

Ghile pulled himself back to his feet and half hopped, half stumbled across the distance between him and his uncle. "Uncle, it's me, Ghile," he said as he fell to the floor by Toren's side.

"Ghile? How... how did you find me? Where are Ecrec and the others?" Toren looked up at him with one good eye. The other had swollen shut. The whole side of Toren's face was one great, bluish black bruise. The light from the fire behind Ghile danced over his uncle's features making them look macabre.

Ghile watched as Riff shot one last blast of flame on Bloody Maw's charred, unmoving corpse.

"Good, dog," Riff said, "Stay." He gingerly sidestepped the flames and walked towards Ghile, his everflame burning before him in an upraised hand.

"I see you found Fang, Toren," Riff stated matter-of-factly. He glanced at the sound of moaning coming from the goblin who still lay on the ground, limply reaching for its chest.

"It is stonechosen," Riff said, walking over to stand above the goblin. He stared down in silence, his face unreadable. Riff slowly extended his hand towards the prone goblin's chest. He moved as if in a dream.

"No, don't," Ghile called. Giving his uncle's shoulder a reassuring squeeze, he pulled himself up and hopped towards Riff.

Riff gingerly touched the skin above the goblin's soulstone, just as Ghile reached him.

Nothing happened.

"It was supposed to be me, Ghile. You were never meant to be in those ruins. Master Almoriz meant for me to find the statue and the seeding stone," Riff said.

"I'm sorry, Riff. I never meant—"

"Can you imagine the power I would have had? Can you?" Riff glared up at Ghile, his eyes hard. The light of the everflame flared briefly. He looked back at the goblin.

Ghile reached down and picked up the goblin's dropped blade. The steel scratched along the stone as he lifted it, awkwardly favoring his good ankle.

Riff turned and rose up to face Ghile.

"Ghile?" Uncle Toren called.

Ghile and Riff stood there for a moment, before Ghile offered him the blade. "Please, free my uncle."

Riff took one more long look at the goblin and his shoulders relaxed as if some weight he had been carrying for a long time finally lifted.

"Better you than me, Sheepherder," Riff said, grinning.

He accepted the knife.

"None too shabby on those other worgs, Ghile. You will have to tell me how you defeated them."

"Ghile, defeated them?" Toren repeated in confusion, looking between his two rescuers.

Riff smirked and went to kneel down beside Toren. "Oh, yes. Haven't you heard? Ghile is a stonechosen of Haurtu. Everyone is talking about it." He set to work on the bonds. Riff carried on explaining everything to Uncle Toren, as if he were chatting about the weather over a cask of Whispering Rock's finest.

Ghile looked down at the small writhing form beneath him. He remembered the pain and disorientation he had felt when he'd been struck by the culler's hammer. He felt sympathy for it as he knelt down. Driven by a feeling, more than anything else, he reached out and moved its small, clawed hands which had curled up to protect the stone. How large it looked in its chest, but Ghile could tell it was identical to his own. He nodded as he took in the suffering creature one last time. He knew once he did this, his path was set and there was no going back. With more calmness than he felt, Ghile reached down and placed his palm over the Goblin's stone.

The cutting pain was sharp and immediate. Unyielding heat seared into his palm. The Goblin's eyes rolled back in its head as it let out a shrilling cry.

Ghile reflexively grabbed the hand attached to the goblin with his other and tried in vain to pull it free. The Goblin was glowing from within, its skin a bright, translucent green. Then it was simply gone, as if it had never existed. With its disappearance, the pain increased in Ghile's hand and he fell back as the new stone began the excruciating journey under his skin towards his chest.

Ghile fought back the urge to pass out. His mind was screaming to give in to the pain and drift off into peaceful oblivion, but Ghile was determined to endure this rite of passage. He felt he owed it to all who had or would suffer for him. He saw both Riff and Toren staring at him, their expressions a mix of curiosity, awe, and fear. His uncle had suffered because of him. Gar was dead. Last Hamlet in danger. All because fate had chosen him.

The stone slid along his shoulder with a sickening, popping sound and Ghile felt cold sweat on his brow, followed by bile rising in his mouth. He turned on his side and vomited.

Laying there, shaking, Ghile saw Two Elks limp into the cavern, supported by Gaidel. He watched as Two Elks dealt with the two worgs whose jaws he had shattered. All strength had left them and they simply lay there whimpering as Two Elks brought his axe down on them in turn.

Ghile smiled weakly. They had defeated the frost wyrm.

Gaidel started towards him, but Riff reached out, stopping her.

The pain finally reached his chest. Ghile heard the sound of meat sizzling on hot stone. He watched Riff trying to reason with Gaidel as she struggled to push past him, but couldn't hear their voices. A scream fought past his gritted teeth and darkness took him.

38

Meeting of the Minds

AGISTER Obudar stood along the parapets of the Bastion, looking out over Lakeside. His mood was as dark as the columns of smoke still rising into the otherwise clear summer sky. Most of the fires had been extinguished, but the few that remained drifted up lazily before being swept out over Crystal Lake by the winds.

He felt a pain in his stomach. He would need to seek out the herbalist for another of his soothing draughts.

He had never thought the humans capable of such an uprising. They had been given everything they needed to be productive members of the empire. He had left them their freedoms and their traditions. He had even armed their fangs with dwarven blades. Was this how they repaid his generosity?

He tightened his fists and pounded on the rough stone in his frustrations, as he counted off lost profits. Word of this would reach the empire and his ability to lead would be questioned. Damn that Knight Justice Finngyr and his hubris! He was the cause of this. If he had only heeded the council's advice and taken that boy into the Bastion to be culled, none of this would have happened.

Obudar watched another patrol of Mother Brambles' druids walk down the center of Market Street, their shieldwardens guarding their flanks. Obudar did not like that he had to depend on the old druid to restore order. He was still suspicious of how they were strangely absent when the Rites of Attrition had occurred and then, when things were at their worst, had arrived en masse to restore order. But, begrudgingly, he had to admit restore order they had.

He looked north up the valley. He wondered what the knight justice would do when he reached Last Hamlet. Obudar feared for the repercussions that would follow. He knew his guards would follow whatever orders they were given. They were good dwarves and loyal to the empire. If the knight justice massacred the people of Last Hamlet, he doubted even the druids could keep the peace. For the first time since coming to the Cradle, the magister truly felt he lived on the edge of civilization. He had to find a way to return things to normal.

The creaking of the stout wooden door announced the arrival of Mother Brambles, escorted by Obudar's steward, Gretchkin.

"His word is law," Obudar greeted them.

Gretchkin quickly responded in kind. Mother Brambles walked over to the parapets, her stick keeping a sharp tapping cadence with her shuffling gait. She stared out over the city for a moment before responding.

"It looks like things have calmed down for now. Any news from Last Hamlet, Magister?"

Gretchkin cleared his throat.

"Thank you, Gretchkin. You may leave us," Obudar said.

Gretchkin bowed his head, turning his palms towards the sky. "Of course, Magister. I will wait for our guest at the stair."

Obudar listened to the swishing of robes until they were silenced by the squeak of the closing door.

The two stood in silence, looking out over the city.

"I have heard nothing from Last Hamlet," Obudar finally said.

"I imagine you are worried this isn't over," Mother Brambles said, without taking her eyes off the view.

Obudar sighed. "If he harms any more of them..."

Mother Brambles did not respond.

"Where were you and the other druids when the Rite of Attrition was held?" Obudar said. He saw no reason for talking around something. It was always best to get straight to the heart of the matter.

"We gathered in council within the Redwood, as we do during every summer festival."

"How very convenient for you to not be present when the culler struck the boy down and the sorcerer conjured those flames and ash to aid in their escape," Obudar said.

Mother Brambles took out her wooden pipe and frowned when she realized there was nowhere to light it. "The sorcerer, you say? I have never known any sorcerer who could control that much flame at one time," Mother Brambles said. She stuck the empty pipe in her mouth and clamped down hard.

"Were all the druids present at your council?" Obudar asked.

Mother Brambles did not seem offended by the question; if she was, the level tone of her reply did not show it. "No druid can guide flame or water, Magister."

"Who then, woman?"

"No one in the Cradle benefits from this madness, be they dwarf or human. I can only assume the one who displayed that power is the one who most benefits from the result," she said. She looked back out over Lakeside and said almost idly, "When do you expect the knight justice to return with the city guard, Magister?"

The aching in Obudar's stomach became a hollow feeling. He had never even once suspected the knight justice. He knew the knight justices had the ability to call on great powers in time of need. If so, then did that mean Daomur himself approved of what was happening? Could the flames and ash have been an attempt to stop the boy from escaping when he had not died from the blow?

Obudar was the first to admit he knew very little of the prophecies. His was a mind for business, not the histories. He knew this boy had to be caught and culled for the good of all, but he did not want what he had built here to be torn down because of it. The more he considered it, the more it made sense. "Daomur's beard, what am I going to do?" Obudar said.

"If by that, you mean what you are going to do about the religious zealot responsible for this mess, I would think the answer was clear. He needs to leave."

Obudar pulled at his beard absently. The ache in his stomach had returned with a vengeance. "By the laws of the empire, the knight justice has control of the Cradle until the boy is captured."

"Or has left the Cradle," Mother Brambles added.

"What did you say?"

"Or has left the Cradle. If the stonechosen leaves the Cradle, then the knight justice leaves with him." Mother Brambles was no longer looking out over Lakeside. Her eyes were focused on the magister like a cat's watching a mouse.

"But how... how would one prove... The knight justice would just tear the Cradle apart looking," Obudar sputtered, his mind racing with thoughts.

"Why the very prophecies that give him the power can also take them away," Mother Brambles said.

Obudar was taken aback. "What do you know of the prophecies?"

Mother Brambles took her pipe from her mouth and poked it towards Obudar with each word she spoke. "The All Mother has no need to have her teachings etched in stone as Daomur does, but that does not mean her faithful are ignorant of them."

Obudar simply stared.

Mother Brambles huffed in exasperation. "You will see the knight justice sooner than you think, Magister. When next you meet, repeat these words to him exactly as I say them to you now. He will leave the Cradle upon hearing them. Then things can return to normal."

Mother Brambles waved her hand out over Lakeside. "All of this nonsense is just bad for business."

Obudar couldn't agree more.

39

Uninvited Guests

HILE awoke on the familiar island beach. The slow lapping water of the lake and warm breeze did not hold the same calming effect they had in the past. He touched his chest and felt the two stones just under his skin.

"Where are you, Adon?" Ghile called, rising. "Or whoever you are."

He strode into the wood. For the first time, he heard a rumble of thunder in his dream paradise. The clouds were darker than he had ever seen them and they swirled with agitation. Ghile could make out his destination; the tall oak, its many limbs swaying in anticipation of the coming storm. He moved through the forest, his hands clenched into tight fists. He caught the movement of the shadow creature from the corner of his eye as it darted from behind one tree to the other, following him. He ignored it. He didn't have time for its games.

"Adon!" He called out. "Come out! Where are you?" Ghile had not been here since the culler had struck him, even though he had tried to enter the dream many times. He was halfway to the oak when he realized he wasn't limping. He gave himself a cursory glance and found no injuries. He took this new information in stride and continued on, ducking under the low branches and walking around the large trunks, the wind whipping debris around him as he went.

The Shadow ran a short distance in front of him and peeked timidly from behind a tree, as it always did. Ghile continued forward, not being veered off the most direct path to the oak, wishing it to attack him this time. But to his disappointment, it again only gestured for him to follow it.

"What do you want? We are alone! Attack me if you're going to," he screamed. He stood there, waiting. Thunder rolled overhead.

The shadow creature cringed behind the tree as he yelled and then, like so many times before, motioned for Ghile to follow.

"Fine!" Ghile said. He reached into his pouch and felt the familiar smoothness of his stones, even though he had used them on the wolves in the waking world. He pulled one out and held it before him, but the shadow creature was already gone. Ghile stood there, his heart pounding, and scanned the forest for the creature. When he was satisfied it was gone, he continued on his way.

Leaves flew around the clearing as Ghile arrived at the great oak. There was Adon, as Ghile had known he would be, sitting on one of the giant roots, waiting. Without forethought, Ghile held up his palm and mind pushed the stone he had drawn for the shadow creature at Adon. The stone flew unerringly at Adon, who sat motionless. At the last moment, the stone hit Adon's force shield and shattered into fine dust.

"Well, hello to you too, little brother," Adon said.

"You are not my brother!" Ghile reached for another stone. Thunder rumbled off the surrounding mountains as the sky darkened further and lighting flashed behind the clouds.

"You need to calm down, Ghile. Why are you attacking me?" Adon said.

Ghile gave up on the idea of hurling another stone. He was just so angry. Fine. No more stones. But he was going to get some answers. "Who are you?" Ghile said.

"You know who I am."

"That is not an answer, Adon." Ghile moved to where he was directly under the root, looking up at Adon.

"Why don't you tell me who you think I am, then?" Adon said.

"Haurtu, the Devourer!" Ghile said. "I think you are the exiled god, trying to return to our world!"

If Ghile's words had any effect, he couldn't see it. Adon was just patiently watching him. "Fine. I'll go along with this. Let's say I'm Haurtu. Now what?" Adon said.

Ghile started to reply several times, stopping each time in turn. That was a very good question. What if he was? Ghile couldn't hurt him, he knew that. He didn't have the power to hurt him. And if Ghile was going to be honest with himself, he had missed him, ever since the culler had struck him. He had missed Adon. He didn't know who this was for certain. If it was Haurtu, then there wasn't much Ghile could do about it now, but go along with him. Ghile closed his eyes and breathed deeply before continuing. "Why couldn't I come here after I was struck by the culler?" Ghile said after a while.

"That blow would have killed you. The stone protected you, but it isn't an easy thing to do. You both needed time to heal," Adon said. He looked up at the clearing sky, and seeming satisfied, pushed off the root, and floated to the ground next to Ghile.

Ghile ran his hand through his hair and sighed. "Nothing for it now, I suppose."

Ghile sat down next to the gnarled root, drawing his knees to his chest. Adon sat down next to him. They both sat there quietly for a time watching as the wind died down and the leaves settled to the forest floor.

Ghile ran his hands over the two lumps in his chest. "How many of these stones are there?" he asked.

Adon, glanced over at him and shrugged. "Don't know."

"When I saw the other stone, I had to have it, Adon. All I could think of was possessing the stone. I even knew how bad the pain was going to be when I took it, but I took it anyway," Ghile said.

Adon nodded, listening. "They call to each other. Now that you have two, if there are others you will be able to feel them, as well. You are stonechosen, Ghile. I have been listening to the Elder's dreamings on this. You must seek out the other stones."

"For they already seek you," a young female voice said.

Ghile had a stone in his hand before he knew he had done it. Adon was faster. A stone shot from his hand, speeding across the clearing, to pass harmlessly through the speaker's translucent body.

The girl was human and not much older than Ghile. She wore a simple gown, the same swirling grey color as she was. She looked like she was made of smoke. If she felt the stone, she did not show it. She walked towards them, never taking her eyes from Ghile.

Ghile suddenly felt the pull of another stone wash over him like the heat from a fire. "You're stonechosen," Ghile said as he jumped to his feet.

"As are you," she replied. Ghile had to concentrate to understand her, she had an odd accent. She moved to stand directly in front of him.

Ghile felt the urge to reach out and place his palm on her chest. She must have felt the same stirrings because her eyes kept moving from where Ghile's stones were embedded, to his eyes.

236

There was something different from the irresistible pull Ghile had felt with the goblin, though. The feeling was somehow less, muted. Ghile tentatively reached out and tried to touch her. As he suspected, his hand simply passed through her.

"How are you doing this?" he asked.

She seemed about to answer, but then noticed the smoke she was composed of start to disperse. "There is no time. I feel the connection slipping. I have never reached this far into the dreaming before, maybe the stones, I don't know. But, I cannot wake."

Her form flowed away quicker. Ghile did not want her to go, he had so many questions. She was stone-chosen like him. "Please, don't go."

"Too far away. Come to the Fallen City. Something is wrong. My brother is..." The girl was gone.

Ghile turned towards Adon. "Where did she go? Have you heard of this city, Adon?"

Adon shook his head, still looking somewhat shocked by the unexpected visitor.

The pull of her stone was all but gone, but he could still feel the tiniest tug deep in his chest. He wondered if it would be enough to lead him to her. She seemed to be in trouble, or her brother was. Ghile knew how upset he would be if his family was in danger.

"Our family! Adon, I have to wake! The culler is going to search for me in Last Hamlet. They are all in danger."

That seemed to snap Adon out of it. "Then you need to wake, Ghile!"

"How?" Ghile tried to remember in the past how he had come out of these dreams. He had always just fallen asleep in this world and awoken in the other. Ghile thought of Tia and shook his head. The worry ate at his gut. There was no way he was going to fall asleep.

"I know how," a voice croaked. Ghile recognized that voice.

He spun around. "What are you doing here, goblin?"

From around the root, skulked the Goblin. Its long ears hung limply on the sides of its oblong head.

"Muk," the Goblin said. "I am Muk." Muk stood before them, its arms hanging at its side, waiting.

Ghile was about to attack it when he noticed it no longer had a stone in its chest. Ghile looked to Adon, but Adon was only staring back at him. Why didn't Adon seem surprised?

"You knew it was here?" Ghile said.

Adon nodded. "He appeared on the ground right where we are standing, only a short time before you came stomping out of the woods."

"Why didn't you say something," Ghile said, throwing his hands in the air.

"You really didn't give me a chance, Ghile. Listen, Muk is here to help you. I think he was brought here as I was," Adon said.

He had no time for this now. "Then tell me how to wake up. Now!" Ghile said.

Muk's ears shot straight up and he began bouncing from foot to foot. "Yes, Muk will teach. I can teach

238

you how to touch animals' minds and have them do your bidding. I can—"

Ghile grabbed the goblin by the shoulders. "I want to know how to wake up!"

Muk winced and then began nodding vigorously. "Yes, Muk teach you." Muk dropped down onto the ground in a sitting position and began breathing deeply. He sucked in great breaths of air and then blew them out with such force, it made Ghile feel light-headed just watching him. Muk opened one eye and then motioned for Ghile to sit down. "You do as Muk do," the floppy-eared Goblin said.

Ghile looked to Adon, who only shrugged. Ghile sat down and began centering himself. He heard Muk croaking out instructions between exaggerated breaths.

"Relax body, starting with feet. Work up slowly to head. All the way up. Feel all body go soft. Then, when ready feel feet sink in ground. Feet heavy. They sink deep. Feel head light like fur drifting on wind. Feel head float up," Muk droned on.

Ghile relaxed his body. This was familiar. He had learned this way of relaxing from Adon. He felt all his muscles release. He forced images of his family from his mind, knowing this was how he could reach them.

Ghile felt his feet getting heavy. They sank into the ground and he felt them spreading out, taking in nourishment. As his head became lighter, he felt it extending upwards into the sky. He felt his hair reaching out like branches. Ghile was the great oak. He could see out over the tiny island. See the circular lake and mountains surrounding it. He could see his roots reaching down forever. He could feel endless possibility above him, but something told him not to go that way. There was confusion there, too many choices.

Somewhere in the distance Ghile heard the croaking of a frog. An incessant chirping was coming from somewhere and he almost lost his focus when he realized it was the Goblin, Muk. "Go down to home," Muk said.

Ghile reached down into his roots, and could feel himself drifting off. He knew this was the way back.

Ghile's sitting body disappeared from beneath the great oak. Adon stood there saying nothing as Muk rose and stared at him in silence.

"Now help me find that shadow," Adon said.

Muk nodded and followed Adon into the woods.

40

Those We Love

HILE bolted up, shocking Gaidel, who had been kneeling next to him. He struggled to rise. His head ached. He tried to swallow, but his mouth was too dry.

"Be at peace, Ghile," Gaidel said. He only struggled for a moment longer before settling for a sitting position. She offered him a small wooden bowl. "Drink this."

At first the water burned, but then it slid down his throat in soothing waves. Who would have thought water could feel so good? Ghile could feel it slide down the sides of his empty stomach. "Hungry," he croaked.

"Well, you should be, Sheepherder. You've been asleep for two days," Riff said.

Riff's annoyingly casual manner made Ghile smile. He was beginning to find it comforting. Then he realized what Riff had said.

"What? No!" Ghile only remembered being on the island for a short time. How he could have been asleep that long? They were still in Muk's cave. He could see a small fire, with their belongings scattered around it. The bodies of the worgs were missing. Sunlight filtered in from the entrance. If he had been asleep for two days Ghile feared the worse for his family. "No, my family! We need to get to Last Hamlet," he said. Ghile started to rise again and almost spilled the large bowl Gaidel was trying to hand him.

Some of whatever was in the new bowl spilled out, burning her fingers, and her visage grew stern. "We are not going anywhere until you eat this. I could barely get you to drink anything and your fever only broke this morning," Gaidel said. She must have seen the argument forming on Ghile's lips. "I will have Two Elks hold you while I pour this down your throat or you can feed yourself," she said. "The choice is yours."

Two Elks moved up behind Gaidel, towering over the both of them. His massive arms crossed over his chest and his raised eyebrow helped emphasize her point.

Ghile took the bowl. "You don't understand. That culler is going to hurt my family."

Gaidel motioned the bowl towards his mouth until Ghile relented and took a sip. It was a meaty soup and

Ghile began scooping more into his mouth, despite his concern.

"Two Elks and Fang Toren returned from Last Hamlet this morning," Gaidel said.

"Are they safe?" Ghile asked as he chewed.

"No one there," Two Elks said. He sat back down to warm his hands by the fire.

Riff dropped down next to Ghile and explained how they had seen smoke rising from Last Hamlet in the morning after his battle against the worgs and goblin. Two Elks and his uncle had set out immediately. When they arrived they found Last Hamlet had been put to the torch, but it was deserted. Even those who had stayed behind when the rest had gone to the summer festival were missing. The two had studied the tracks and could tell the dwarves had arrived to an empty village and could only assume they burned it in their frustrations. Their tracks led back down the valley.

Burning a village in frustration did not sound like something the dwarves would do. But then, Ghile remembered the look in the culler's eyes and knew he was fully capable of such an action. "Where are they, then?" Ghile said.

"My guess is Master Almoriz gathered the remaining villagers and took them down the valley to meet up with those coming up from Lakeside. I think he would have taken them somewhere the dwarves would not think to look," Riff said.

Ghile was sure the dwarves would be searching in every village and hamlet in both Upper and Lower

Vale. He couldn't think of any place where you could hide an entire village, except …. "The ruins," Ghile said.

"Exactly. Your uncle set out from Last Hamlet yesterday to find them and let Master Almoriz and your family know you were alive," Riff said.

"He is a skilled tracker," Two Elks added from his place by the fire.

"Wait – Uncle Toren didn't look able to stand," Ghile said. He remembered his uncle, bound and lying wounded on the ground next to Muk.

"I healed him," Gaidel said.

Ghile remembered his mauled leg. He moved it gingerly, waiting for the sharp pain and resulting nausea, but it didn't come. Instead, there was only a dull ache and stiffness in the joints. He reached up and touched his shoulder where the arrow had grazed him. There was no pain there, either. He suddenly felt his face redden. Gaidel had healed him as well and had been tending him while he laid helpless on the floor. "Thank you for helping us, Gaidel," Ghile said. He dug into the bowl of stew she had given him. The least he could do was be a good patient.

Gaidel swallowed and averted her eyes.

Ghile worried he had somehow offended her. "Daughter Gaidel, I mean."

As quickly as the look had come, it disappeared from her face and she smiled at him. "No, Ghile. It isn't that. Please, call me Gaidel." She seemed to be struggling with what to say, or at least how to say it. "I did not heal your wounds," she finally said.

Ghile tested his ankle again, confused. "Then how?"

"Your wounds mended themselves while you slept," Gaidel said. "I don't really understand how, I had tried to sing their healing, but..." She averted her eyes again.

Ghile couldn't help but think she looked scared.

"It is good you are healed, Ghile Stonechosen," Two Elks rose and walked up to Ghile, handing him a circular chord with long, yellowed teeth hanging from it. "You fought well. Wear this, so others know you are warrior," Two Elks said.

Ghile looked from the barbarian to the necklace. It was made of stretched skin and worg fangs. There was still blood and small flecks of flesh on some of the teeth. He resisted the urge to withdraw his hand, lest he offend Two Elks and gingerly took the necklace. "Thank you."

Two Elks nodded. For some reason Ghile felt proud in pleasing Two Elks.

Riff patted Ghile on the back. "Just be glad it wasn't a paw on the end of a stick or something," he whispered.

"Now we leave this place. The Cradle is not safe," Two Elks said.

"What? No, we cannot leave yet," Ghile said.

"Ghile, as long as you remain in the Cradle, you are not safe," Gaidel said.

"You all agreed to help me find my uncle so I could speak with him and see that my family was safe. Until I speak with him and actually see my family, I refuse to leave the Cradle." Ghile swallowed back the rest of what he was going to say. The three of them had already risked their lives. He knew they were only trying to protect him. He was acting like a spoiled child again. He ran his hand through his hair and squeezed the back of his neck. "Look, I'm sorry. Thank you for helping me save my uncle," Ghile started. He looked to Riff, "and for saving me," he added.

Riff winked at him, smiling.

"I know we need to leave the Cradle. I even know where we need to go." He raised his hand when he saw their expressions change. There would be time to explain about the girl and the Fallen City later. "Please understand I may never see them again." So many emotions bubbled just below the surface threatening to boil over. "I need to say goodbye," Ghile said.

Ghile could feel something pass between them in the moment that followed as they all stood in that cave on the side of the Horn. For Ghile, it felt as if their destinies had just intertwined.

"To the ruins then," Gaidel finally said, breaking the silence.

"Have another bowl of Two Elks' worg stew, Ghile," Riff said.

Ghile pulled a face as he stared down at his bowl. "This is worg?"

"Delicious, isn't it?" Riff said, grinning.

41

It is Written

INNGYR stormed into the magister's meeting hall. He dragged the young apprentice, Bjurst, by the hair and gave the miserable excuse of a servant a final shake for good measure before hurling him forward onto the floor.

"What is this beardling prattling on about, Magister?" Finngyr demanded. He was in a foul mood. He had not landed on the roof of the Bastion but ten minutes ago. He had not been able to find the Hungering God's vessel, or any humans for that matter, in that wretched little village. On top of that, it looked like the humans of Lakeside had decided to behave themselves. Finngyr had seen them going on about their normal lives when he flew over the town. He had been itching to help quell any rebellion. He was in a foul mood indeed.

The magister and the other clan elders were all seated at the low stone table, looking smug. If Finngyr didn't know better, he would have sworn they looked as if they were waiting for him.

He didn't have time for this nonsense.

"When I ordered him to send for a runesmith, he told me I was to be immediately escorted before this council." Finngyr all but spat the words, each one louder than the one before.

"Which he did admirably. Thank you, Bjurst. You may go," the magister said.

Finngyr couldn't believe his ears. Had this coin mongering fool finally lost all good sense? Why were they all sitting there so glibly? Finngyr resisted the urge to kick the apprentice as Bjurst scrambled up and bowed his way out the door. "What are you about, Magister? Do you need to be reminded who is in charge? There is a vessel of the Hungering God somewhere in this settlement that the empire has entrusted you to oversee. Summon a runesmith to send a message to Daomount. I am going to need help if I'm to find that cursed whelp. Those poor excuses for guards you have cannot even find an entire village!"

The magister motioned and one of the young human children they used as messengers ran forward. "Send runners into Upper and Lower Vale. Tell Sergeant Montul to return to the Bastion." He sent the boy running with a quick pat on the head.

Finngyr had had enough. He was going to tear the magister apart with his bare hands. "You dare usurp me? You deny the rights given to me by the Prophecies!" He started forward, his gauntleted hands clenching into fists.

Magister Obudar rose from his seat to slam his fists down on the cold, unmoving table. "It is by the Prophecies that I resume control of the Cradle, Knight Justice!"

Finngyr continued his advance. "What does someone like you know of the Prophecies?"

The magister began speaking words that Finngyr recognized as a direct quote from the Book of Hjurl. That stopped him. He had just been a beardling himself when he first read those runes. It brought back many memories of the temple of Daomur where he spent his youth on the highest summits of Daomount.

> *"Now marked his chosen must gather*
> *Where once his progeny thrived*
> *His hunger compels them to journey*
> *In his cities they survive."*

"You cannot find the boy because he is no longer in the Cradle, Knight Justice. It is known the only ancient human dwellings in the Cradle are those tiny ruins at the base of the Horn. Hardly what one would call a city. Every day you spend here looking under rocks, is another day that boy grows stronger and gets closer to his destination," the magister said.

Finngyr stood there rigid, staring at each of those fat merchants. As much as it pained him to admit it, the magister was right. How could he have forgotten what was written in the Prophecies on the trials of the vessels? It was why their ruins were forbidden. He would need to consult the book of Hjurl to see what else he might learn. How far had the boy already gotten? Which of the human cities would he seek? "How do you know runes from the Book of Hjurl so well, Magister? Do you have engravings here?" Finngyr begrudgingly asked.

The magister sat back down and looked to the other elders before replying. "We are but a small outpost on the very edge of the empire, Knight Justice. We would not have such engravings here."

Finngyr fought the anger down. As he looked upon the serene faces of the other dwarves, he realized how he must appear to them. All dwarves were taught from an early age that emotions clouded judgments. Daomur's laws were to be weighed in a clear mind. Maybe he was the one who had spent too much time with these tainted humans. He took a steadying breath. "Then I shall take my leave, Magister. The Temple thanks you for granting hospitality to one of its brethren. The Cradle is yours," Finngyr recited.

"His word is law," the magister intoned, followed by the rest at the table.

"His word is law," Finngyr repeated, bowing his head slightly. He turned to leave.

"Knight Justice, what of your prisoner?" the magister called.

It took Finngyr a moment before he recalled who the magister was asking about. "Do what you will with that fat sorcerer. He is of no more interest to me," Finngyr said as he left the hall.

42

To be Chosen

 HILE sat on the dusty floor of what he now realized was a hidden shrine to a stonechosen of Haurtu. He absently nursed his ankle. It was still stiff from their descent down the Horn. Two everflame torches filled the small circular room with light, causing shadows to dance along the carvings in the surrounding walls. The wooden debris he remembered had been cleared. The human statue still stood where he remembered it, tall and straight near the opposite wall. He split his gaze between the stone spiral in its chest and the statue's conceit-filled stare.

Ghile thought a look of terror might have been more appropriate. *Maybe if the ancient sculptor actually knew what destiny lay before a stonechosen, he would have carved a look that would have warned*

people to stay away from it? The thought made him chuckle.

"What do you find funny?" Master Almoriz asked from where he sat on the stone stairs leading up and out of the hidden room. Those were the first words shared between the two since Uncle Toren had brought him here.

Uncle Toren had met them outside the ruins where he had been hidden and on guard near one of the many entrances. Ghile was still confused by the way his uncle had greeted them. The smile his uncle usually shared with him was gone, replaced by a thin-lipped, no nonsense look.

He had spoken quietly with Gaidel first, which bothered Ghile more than he cared to admit, before asking Ghile to follow him. He had not answered any of Ghile's questions, only saying Master Almoriz would explain. He was then taken on a roundabout path through the ruins to the same angled room with the multiple exits and the shaft of light shining down on the square hole.

Because of the way his uncle had treated him, and being brought to the very room where his trouble began, a room they had denied even existed, Ghile had said nothing and sat down to stare angrily at the Sorcerer of Whispering Rock, who, frustratingly, seemed more than willing to wait.

"You lied to me," Ghile said.

"Not even the pretense of manners now, I see, Ghile of Last Hamlet."

"There is no more Last Hamlet," Ghile said. He resisted the urge to add, "Because of me". Even though it was the culler who had actually burned his home, none of this would have happened had he not come down into this room and touched that statue. "I am Ghile Stonechosen, now."

"So you are, so you are," Master Almoriz said.

Ghile heard the change in the sorcerer's tone. For the first time, Master Almoriz sounded old. He was obviously old, but he had never seemed it.

But now Ghile could hear it in his voice. Ghile was not the only one affected. Master Almoriz had caused those fires to erupt at the Rite of Attrition, killing and wounding all those people, just so Ghile could escape. "I am sorry, Master Almoriz," Ghile finally said after a long stretch of silence.

"No, you are right. I have some explaining to do," Master Almoriz said. He glanced up towards the top of the stairs and then seeming satisfied, moved to sit next to Ghile along the wall. He made more than a few complaints about aches and old bones as he settled onto the floor and leaned back carefully. "We have time before we go meet with your family." He seemed to take a moment to compose himself and then cleared his throat. "What I share with you now has not been shared with any but a select few outside my order, Ghile Stonechosen. Know I only share it with you now, because of what you are and because I think it might help keep you alive."

"We sorcerers do not share the true extent of our knowledge and true purpose. There are many secrets we have passed down through the ages from master to apprentice. If the dwarves saw us as more than useful tinkerers, they would have eradicated us long ago. We are not offered the same protections that druids are under dwarven laws," Master Almoriz said.

Ghile thought about what secrets Riff might be keeping. "Even the Sorcerer of Lakeside?" Ghile asked.

Master Almoriz wrinkled up his face, engulfing his mouth in whiskers. "There are, unfortunately, some who would rather grow fat and actually become what the dwarves think us to be," Master Almoriz said. "Those still loyal to our beliefs actively watch the stars and seek the Soulstones of Haurtu." Master Almoriz motioned at the statue. "Those stones in his chest. Much like the one you now have."

"Two," Ghile corrected.

"What?" Master Almoriz asked, his eyebrows coming to life and racing up his forehead.

Ghile took a deep breath and went on to explain about the encounter on the Horn. Ghile found once he got started, he couldn't stop. Everything that had happened to him came pouring out. He spoke of Adon and his dream teachings. How Muk was now there and wished to teach him as well. He even told Master Almoriz about the strange girl who had appeared and spoken of the Fallen City.

Master Almoriz listened patiently and only interrupted to clarify a point or to add a, "go on", or an, "I see".

When Ghile finished, he realized his cheeks were wet with tears. He did not know when he had started crying. He hastily wiped them away.

"Our people have lost so much knowledge, Ghile," Master Almoriz said. "I have never heard any stories about a type of limbo for those who died during the Great Purge and those who have been culled since, but that could explain why there are so few of us since then. Disturbing news if it is true."

"Do you think it really is Adon, Master Almoriz?"

"I honestly do not know. Mother Brambles told me she taught you our histories as we know them. You will be taught more with each soulstone you acquire. With each soulstone, your strength and knowledge will grow. How this knowledge is shared with you, the histories do not say. But, when it comes to the gods, I would not rule any possibility out."

Ghile hoped it was really Adon. The idea that because of him, his brother was able to escape from that limbo and reside in his dreams, was comforting.

"But understand this, Ghile, Haurtu's way is the strongest survive and the weak perish. It is through the stonechosen that Haurtu may return. You will be tested. The stones call to each other. Only one of the stonechosen will become the key that releases Haurtu. You will need to be strong to survive the trials to come," Master Almoriz said. "The barbarians of the Nordlah Plains have great contests of skill and combat to determine who among them is fit to seek the soulstones. It is a great honor among their people. It is why they resist the dwarven yoke and openly war with them."

Ghile wondered what Two Elks thought of him. What a waste he must seem to the barbarian. Ghile realized something else then. "All those times you sent Riff into these ruins. You wanted him to find a soulstone."

Master Almoriz nodded.

"He can have it!" Ghile quickly said. "I never asked for any of this. Can you not use your powers and take it from me?"

Master Almoriz sighed. "Once you are stonechosen there is no turning back, Ghile. I am sorry this happened to you, lad, I surely am. The stars were finally right for the return of the soulstones and I hoped one might appear somewhere in this ancient temple. Your choices are few, I'm afraid. Become the key to Haurtu's release or have your soulstone taken from you as you lie on the brink of death by another stonechosen."

Ghile didn't care for either of those two choices. "What if I die before either of those things happen?" Ghile said.

"The soulstones will prevent that from happening. Have you not noticed your body now heals itself, of even the gravest of wounds?" Master Almoriz said.

Ghile touched his ankle where the worg had savaged him. He remembered feeling the beast's fangs scrape against his bone. Only two days had passed since then and all that remained was some stiffness. He thought of the flash of light when the culler had struck him and the same light when he had struck Muk with a force stone. He asked as much and Master Almoriz nodded vigorously.

"Those wounds were death blows. The soulstones protect you even from those fatal wounds. But, even the soulstones have their limits. The stonechosen are at their weakest then, as both they and the soulstones must recover. That is the only time one stonechosen can draw a soulstone from another," Master Almoriz said.

As Master Almoriz talked, Ghile thought back to the two times he had taken on a soulstone. The pain of the stone crawling, almost bug-like, just under his flesh and then burning itself into his chest. Bile began to seep into his throat. He slid his tongue across his teeth, swallowing thickly.

"Do not think this makes you immortal, Ghile Stonechosen. If you do not eat or drink, you will waste away like any of us, but you will not die. I would hate to experience such a fate."

"As would I," Ghile said.

"I said there were only two ways, but I left out your fate if you are captured by the cullers. Though the histories do not tell us their fate, no stonechosen ever captured by the cullers has ever been heard from again," Master Almoriz said. "I think you also realize now that you must dream to learn. You also must sleep to recover from severe wounds. You cannot protect yourself at all times. This is why I have asked my apprentice to accompany you on your journey, as well as the young druid and her shieldwarden."

"How many of us are there?" Ghile said, trying to think on something else.

"That is the one thing none can agree on. It is not known. Though I think there must be at least four," Master Almoriz stated.

"Why do you say that?" Ghile said.

Master Almoriz motioned towards the statue looking down at them. A series of four stones formed the beginning of a spiraling pattern in the statue's chest. Ghile wondered who this stonechosen had been. Why had this shrine been built for him? Ghile wondered if he had been honored, or hated among his people. He thought about the way his uncle had acted towards him. What did his uncle think about him now? What about his parents? "Why did my uncle separate me from my companions and sneak me into the ruins to see you, Master Almoriz?" Ghile asked.

Master Almoriz blinked and looked away from the statue. He must have been deep in thought because it took him a moment to respond. "Your uncle?"

"I would like to see my family now," Ghile said.

43

Goodbyes

HEY stood at one of the southern entrances into the old ruins. The sun's late afternoon rays climbed up the valley like clinging fingers, trying to find some purchase in the deep crevasses of the windswept stone in a vain attempt to keep the sun from sinking below the horizon.

Ghile watched its slow descent toward the tops of the distant Redwood. Once it set, they would begin their journey. Ghile had so often dreamed of leaving the Cradle of the Gods. He always pictured himself striding gallantly out of Lakeside on some great adventure, all the gathered villagers cheering and waving as he went.

Instead, he was sneaking out after dark, taking one of the few hunting trails that skirted around the mountain side of Crystal Lake and down out of the

Cradle along one of the many rivers that flowed into the Ghost Fens.

The others had decided it was a more direct route towards their destination and they were less likely to be seen going that way. Ghile could feel the ever-so-slight tug of the girl's soulstone in that direction and knew they were right on both counts.

But, he also knew there were good reasons no one used that way to leave the Cradle. Places like the Ghost Fens didn't get those names without good reason. In addition, even if they made it through the fens there was nothing beyond but the Deepwoods, domain of the elves.

Almoriz had heard of the Fallen City and knew that it was located in the middle of the elven forests, not too far from another human settlement like the Cradle. The settlement was their first destination where they were to seek out a tradesman named Dagbar.

Master Almoriz stood to the side with Riff, going through his pouches and over the many things Riff was supposed to remember. Riff listened intently, nodding occasionally and seeming impatient to be on his way.

Ghile had not had a chance to speak with him since his talk with Master Almoriz. Now that he knew Riff was meant to be stonechosen, he somehow felt he owed him an apology or something.

Two Elks leaned against one of the nearby rocky outcroppings, his stone axe and huge shield next to him. Even now, he was watching their surroundings for any threat. Gaidel knelt near him, going through their provisions and trying to balance them among the many packs. She had not spoken to Ghile since the cave and Ghile had seen her staring at him from the corner of his eye, more than once. He would have to find time to talk with her later.

Ghile reached down and picked up Tia to hug her one more time, trying to commit the feeling to memory. He wondered how big she would be when he saw her next. He hoped he would see her and his family again.

His mother had not stopped crying since Master Almoriz had brought Ghile to them. Her eyes were red and puffy as she watched her remaining two children together, her face a mixture of pain and pride. Ghile had hoped to say goodbye to some of the others from his hamlet, but many of them blamed him for their present situation, Gar's father Dargen chief among them.

This didn't bother Ghile as much as he would have thought, probably because a part of him had to agree. His father, on the other hand, had not stopped complaining about the fickleness of some of their relatives and wouldn't be returning to Last Hamlet to rebuild. He said what the dwarves had done could not stand and many of the others agreed, including Uncle Toren.

Elana stepped forward and hugged Ghile and Tia. "I just got you back and I am losing you again."

Ghile set Tia down. She took her mother's hand and looked between her and Ghile. She didn't seem to understand what was truly happening, but knew her mother was upset. She bit her lower lip and reached for Elana, who scooped her up quickly. Ghile was glad his mother still had Tia.

"Take this," Ecrec said, stepping up and handing Ghile his spear. "Remember everything I taught you, Son." His eyes had that same serious look he had during lessons that demanded you pay attention.

Ghile nodded. "Thank you, Father. I will."

Uncle Toren stepped up next to Ecrec and handed Ghile something wrapped in furs. Ghile's breath caught when he saw it was his uncle's fighting knife, the one he'd received after becoming a Fang of the Cradle. The long blade was steel and curved into a point. The handle made from deer antler, Ghile could see the thick rounded end where it had fallen off during a molt.

"Uncle, I couldn't," Ghile started to say.

"No, Ghile. You will have need of it more than I. Two Elks can train you how to use it. Fangs were given those to help protect the Cradle. They are enchanted by the dwarves. Ecrec told me Mother Brambles chose you as a fang. It appears the All Mother has chosen you for something even more. You deserve it," his uncle said.

Ghile took the blade and felt the weight of it. It was heavier than he had expected.

"Thank you, Uncle. Thank you, Father," Ghile said.

"I am proud of you, Son," Ecrec said.

Ghile swallowed hard and chose to simply nod. How long had he wanted to hear those words? His eyes burned as he fought back the tears he knew would flow freely if he tried to speak. He felt a hand on his shoulder.

"It is time," Master Almoriz said.

Ghile nodded. *Thank you for saving me*, he thought. The others had already gathered and were putting on and shifting the weight of their packs. Gaidel handed Ghile his and he slid it onto his shoulders and tried to balance the weight.

Two Elks and Gaidel were already making their way down the rocky slope, Riff close behind, his everflame dancing in his open palm. Ghile hurried to catch up. His new vision allowed him to see as well in the twilight as if it was the middle of the day.

Behind him he heard the two Valehounds barking. Ghile turned and felt a sudden need to call to them. They had never listened to him before and had even gone out of their way to torment him, but they were a piece of his past and he wanted them with him.

"Ast! Cuz! To Me!" Ghile said.

The two dogs continued to bark, but did not leave Ecrec's side. Ghile could see his father's face clearly and saw him glance down at the two dogs and then back at Ghile. His father couldn't know how clearly Ghile could see him. He was nodding.

Ghile thought back to his dream and remembered what Muk had said. *Yes, Muk will teach. I can teach you how to touch animals' minds and have them do your bidding.*

Ghile hadn't had any dream training, but the stone was there, firmly in his chest. Now was as good a time as ever. Clearing his mind, Ghile concentrated

264

on Ast and Cuz and tried extending his consciousness out to them. At first he felt nothing, but then something small. It was barely perceptible, that feeling Ghile sometimes got when he was being watched or when there was someone right behind him. It was weak, but it was there.

He knew something was happening because both Valehounds sat up straighter and focused on him. Cuz tilted his head to the side and gave a whine. "Ast! Cuz! To me!" Ghile said

A proud smile appeared on Ecrec's face when both hounds bounded up and ran towards Ghile. They each circled around him once and then settled into a sitting position on either side of him as Ghile had seen them do for his father so many times before. "I'm not a wolf, but a fine lesson all the same, right boys?" Ghile said, ruffling their fur.

Ghile looked back to his father. Ecrec nodded and put an arm around Elana, pulling her and Tia close. "Take care of him, boys," Ecrec called.

Ghile shouldered his pack and, with Ast and Cuz at his side, followed his new companions into the gloaming.

Dear reader,

We hope you enjoyed reading *Cradle of the Gods*. Please take a moment to leave a review, even if it's a short one. Your opinion is important to us.

Discover more books by Thomas Quinn Miller at https://www.nextchapter.pub/authors/thomas-quinn-miller-fantasy-author

Want to know when one of our books is free or discounted? Join the newsletter at http://eepurl.com/bqqB3H

Best regards,
Thomas Quinn Miller and the Next Chapter Team

Name Pronunciation & Race Guide

Humans

Adon \\'ā-'dən\\
Almoriz \\'al-mə-'riz\\
Ecrec \\'ek-rik\\
Elana \\i-'lə-'na\\
Gaidel \\gī-del\\
Ghile \\'gē-lā\\
Two Elks \\'tü-elks\\

Dwarves

Finngyr \\'fin-gir\\
Obudar \\'ō-bə-där\\

Goblins

Goblin Muk \\'mək\\

About the Author

Thomas grew up in a small town in Illinois where he spent most of his time enjoying scouting and playing role playing games. After graduation he joined the military, obtained a degree in Computer Science and saw the world. Since leaving the military, his job in IT continues to keep him abroad. As of the completion of this book, he hangs his hat in a small town in England, with his lovely wife and children, where he can be found spending most of his time enjoying scouting and playing role playing games. Some things never change.

Cradle of the Gods
ISBN: 978-4-86747-196-8 (Mass Market)

Published by
Next Chapter
1-60-20 Minami-Otsuka
170-0005 Toshima-Ku, Tokyo
+818035793528
20th May 2021